THE BEAU
AND THE
BLUESTOCKING

Alice Chetwynd Ley

SAPERE
BOOKS

THE BEAU
AND THE
BLUESTOCKING

Published by Sapere Books.

11 Bank Chambers, Hornsey, London, N8 7NN,
United Kingdom

saperebooks.com

ISBN: 978-1-912546-97-8

Chapter I

Almack's Assembly Rooms in King Street had nothing particularly to recommend them in the way of splendid interior decorations, appointments or hangings. The refreshments served there were, in the words of one disgusted young male visitor to town, positively shabby; small cakes, tea, and nothing more alcoholic than orgeat or lemonade. In spite of this, however, during the London season the Rooms were always filled with the flower of the town's young ladies and the most eligible of its bachelors. The Marriage Mart, Almack's was sometimes unkindly named, especially by those who for one reason or another were unable to obtain vouchers. For admission to this unpretentious place of entertainment was one of the most jealously guarded privileges.

There were those whose welcome was assured and who had been attending the Assemblies for many years. Among these was Mrs Olivia Manbury, wife of Thomas Manbury, M.P., and a well-known fashionable hostess. On a certain evening in spring in the early 1780s, she was sitting in the ballroom with one of her married daughters, Lady Fothergill, closely studying one of the couples who were dancing, a slight frown of disapproval on her brow.

There could have been nothing in the appearance of the pair to raise censure in the most critical eye. The girl was attractively dressed in a gown of straw-coloured silk embroidered with small pink flowers. She was young and graceful, with a heart-shaped face framed by dark curls, lustrous brown eyes and a dimpling smile which never failed to captivate the gentlemen. Her partner, too, was outstandingly personable and elegant in satin knee breeches and an impeccably cut coat of claret velvet. Yet more than one significant glance was turned in their direction; a fact which, though they gave no sign of it, did not escape the notice of either.

Caroline Fothergill laughed softly. 'You look uncommon put out, Mama, considering that Lydia's partnered by one of the most eligible bachelors in the room.'

'Eligible fiddlesticks! What does that signify when a man's as accomplished a flirt as Devenish? You know as well as I do that he means nothing by it. Why, I've watched him paying attentions to a score of girls over the past few years, and just when everyone thinks he must be serious at last, off he goes to a new flirt! The most determined husband hunters have quite given him up — I heard Lady Guiting say the other day that she doubted if he would ever wed at all, and you know how persistent she can be on behalf of those four daughters of hers. Not unattractive girls, either,' added Mrs Manbury, determined to be fair. 'But without dowries, they can scarcely hope — however that is nothing to the purpose. I don't care to see Lydia wasting her time on Devenish.'

'I wouldn't have said that she was,' remarked Caroline, surveying her sister critically. 'She appears to be enjoying herself — as well she may, because every other female of marriageable age in the room is casting her envious glances.'

'More fools they!' retorted Mrs Manbury.

'Oh, I don't know. Beau Devenish may not be the marrying kind, but his attentions are worth cultivating, all the same. He's one of those rare men who know how to make a woman feel that she's irresistible. Only see how Lydia sparkles! But you wouldn't understand of course.'

'You need not suppose, my dear Caroline,' said Mrs Manbury, bridling a little, 'that just because I am the mother of three grown girls — well, young women, if you like — I am therefore totally impervious to male charm. I am well aware of the satisfaction your sister must feel in being singled out for the attentions of such a man as Sir James Devenish. But I am afraid for her — afraid that she may make the mistake of taking him seriously, for one thing —'

'What, Lydia lose her heart to him?' asked Caroline cynically. 'Mama, you must know her better than that — I doubt very much if she has a heart to lose.'

'Come, come, that's a hard thing to say of your sister! She's a sensible girl, I know, and not likely to throw her bonnet over the windmill,' replied Mrs Manbury, tacitly acknowledging the justice of these sisterly reflections. 'But there are other evils. While Devenish flirts with her, it holds off more serious suitors — Calver, for instance, and Bedwyn.'

'The Duke of Bedwyn?' echoed Caroline, incredulously. 'Mama, you would never promote a match between Lydia and that horrid old man?'

Mrs Manbury glanced about her apprehensively. 'Hush! Someone may hear you.' Then in a lower tone, 'Certainly I would. Lydia a Duchess, with a vast estate in Lincolnshire, besides two smaller country houses elsewhere, not to speak of the town house! And a fortune to match! I should be sadly lacking in my maternal duty if I didn't make a push to secure such an establishment for her.'

'Your maternal duty — oh, yes.' Caroline's mouth, which in repose tended to have a discontented droop, now twisted scornfully. 'You mustn't neglect that, as you exercised it so successfully on my own behalf.'

Mrs Manbury shot her a suspicious glance. 'I know you mean to be odiously sarcastic but nevertheless you must own that I chose what seemed best for you at the time. After all, how could we have known that within six years Stapleton would rise from a mere sub-lieutenant to the rank of Rear-Admiral, and moreover, come into a handsome fortune from his grandfather? Such accidents,' she said, complainingly, 'quite overthrow one's most careful calculations. But it's turned out well enough, Caroline. You are even better off financially than you would have been as Stapleton's wife, and you have a title into the bargain.'

'Do you ever consider, Mama, what I have lost?'

Mrs Manbury looked for a moment into her daughter's eyes, and felt vaguely uneasy at what she saw there.

'Oh, some boy and girl nonsense of course.' She spoke briskly. 'But that soon goes, and then one is left with the harsh realities of life — how to keep up a respectable style of living on an insufficient income. Besides Fothergill is a good husband, is he not? He doesn't womanise or gamble away his fortune —'

'Oh, no. He has no extravagant vices. Our life is a model of domestic bliss. When we are neither entertaining nor being entertained — and fortunately that is seldom — he takes a glass or two of port after dinner, and we sit one each side of the fireplace, I with my needlework or a book, and he snoring fit to raise the rafters.'

'Well so it is with all husbands. What would you have, my dear?' Caroline shrugged, but made no reply. 'I fear that in spite of six years of marriage and two children, you're still a romantic schoolgirl. I only hope Lydia has more sense.'

'Oh, yes, Lydia has sense — if that's what you call sense, Mama. She's not in the least romantic. She's like you. I dare say she'll be very willing to marry Bedwyn, and realise your fondest hopes. And she'll have the advantage of never knowing what she's missed.'

'Really, you're talking very strangely tonight. I cannot understand you.' Mrs Manbury glanced at her daughter again. 'You haven't been quarrelling with Fothergill, have you?'

Caroline laughed harshly. 'There's not sufficient real feeling in our relationship to spark off a quarrel,' she said bitterly. 'But don't let us speak any more of me and my concerns. Tell me how you go on with my cousin Alethea. Why isn't she here tonight?'

'She has gone to Montagu House with Miss Hannah More,' replied Mrs Manbury, in tones of disapproval.

'To see the Queen of the Bluestockings?' asked Caroline, with a little more animation. 'But why do you sound so disgruntled about that, Mama? There can be no possible objection to her visiting in such a respectable quarter, and, I may say, under the chaperonage of a lady of such high moral tone!'

'Of course not. But it was not to cultivate Alethea's bookish tendencies that my sister Newnham sent her to me. Her notion was to give the girl a little town polish and to see if I could put her in the way of making a suitable match. I promised to do what I could, for Cassandra is my only sister, and the girl's my godchild. No one shall say I am lacking in family feeling. But things have been a little more difficult than I supposed.'

'Oh, indeed. Why?'

'Well, for one thing, Lydia does not take to her cousin. They are very different in temperament, of course — that was only to be expected, with Alethea's unorthodox upbringing. The only girl among a family of six boys, and educated by her father in exactly the same way as her brothers, from an early age! As you must know, Newnham is a prodigiously scholarly man of unworldly opinions — as I dare say a clergyman ought to be,' added Mrs Manbury dubiously. 'Though you would think well-to-do parents such as the Newnhams would make some push to give a girl an elegant education befitting her sex. Of course, she did spend the last few years at a school for girls managed by Miss Hannah More's sisters at Bristol; but if only Cassandra had applied to me earlier, I would have directed her to Madame Clarke-Wyndham's Seminary, where you three girls all received such a superior education.'

'Only think what benefits she's missed,' commented Caroline wryly. 'My skill at embroidery is well known, everyone agrees that my dancing is most graceful, and I can enter and dismount from a carriage as elegantly as any female in town!'

'You may mock, but such things are more important to a female than being able to read Latin and Greek, or poring for hours over Shakespeare. Accomplishments of that kind,' pronounced Mrs Manbury with authority, 'won't help any girl to get a husband — far from it, for men do not like females to be bookish. Indeed, if a girl knows where her interest lies, she will always contrive to appear a little more stupid than she actually is — certainly more so than the man she intends to marry.'

'It would be difficult to appear more stupid than George.'

'Upon my word, you are very severe on your husband! I am sure there's no more amiable creature alive. He always attends to what you say, which is more than your Papa does to me, and at all times tries his best to please you. Really, Caroline, I don't know what more you want.'

Caroline stifled a yawn. 'Perhaps I don't know myself. But tell me more about my cousin Alethea.'

'There's little enough to tell, as she's scarce been with us a se'ennight. She has some odd ways — only imagine, she reads your father's newspaper, and attempts to talk to him of politics and the like! Even I myself would not venture so far, and it certainly seems odd in a young girl.'

Caroline smiled, for once not unkindly. 'And how does Papa take it?'

'Oh, he seems amused. I am relieved to find him so disposed to be indulgent, for at first I feared he might be vexed. She does not scruple to express her opinions, you know, and Papa is not used to being contradicted. Well, what man is, in his own home? But I fancy that matters are vastly different in my sister Newnham's household. We have rarely paid them visits, but on the few occasions when we've stayed at their home in Somerset, I remember being amazed at the freedom allowed in that way to the children. It seemed to me that my brother-in-law positively encouraged them to air their own views on any and every topic.' Mrs Manbury shook her head decisively. 'Such an upbringing cannot be other than harmful, in my opinion. Young people need to be given a firm sense of direction, and be taught to respect the views of those who are older and wiser than themselves.'

'Perhaps so,' replied Caroline, thoughtfully. 'When you brought Alethea to see me, I must say I was quite taken with her, though. She's unusually direct for a female, I admit, but she has no trace of arrogance or self-assertiveness. One cannot find any fault with her manners, either. She talked for several minutes to George's old Aunt Berengaria, whom as a rule everyone ignores because she is such a tedious bore. Aunt B was singing her praises after you'd gone. She thought Alethea a pretty girl, she said, and so considerate to her elders.'

'Pretty? I wouldn't say so. She is nothing to Lydia, or to what you and Eleanor were at that age. Her figure is not unpleasing, and she has delicate features with a certain sweetness of expression, I grant you. But what man will be likely to send a glance in her direction while Lydia is in the same room? And that is another of the difficulties I am faced with in trying to find the girl a husband.'

'Well, then, Mama, I can see only two alternatives before you. Either Alethea must remain a spinster, or else we must see to it that Lydia becomes engaged at the earliest possible moment.'

'Nothing would please me more than to see your sister betrothed — to someone suitable, of course. But only tell me how it is to be achieved while she persists in permitting Devenish to flirt with her in that outrageous way?'

Chapter II

If Almack's Assembly Rooms could have been described as the hub of fashionable London, Mrs Elizabeth Montagu's new house in Portman Square was the centre of the literary set. This was no recent event. For more than twenty years the 'Queen of the Bluestockings', as she had once been dubbed, had gathered about her in her former house in Hill Street, a coterie of writers, painters and actors which included some of the foremost names of the day. Dr Johnson had come regularly to her soirees until a recent disagreement between them about Lord Lyttleton's work. Goldsmith, Sheridan and David Garrick had rubbed shoulders there with the brilliant Charles James Fox, Gibbon the historian and Adam Smith the economist; Sir Joshua Reynolds was a frequent visitor, while of late years the talented novelist Miss Fanny Burney and the more sober Hannah More had joined the Bas Bleu circle.

Informality was the keynote of these gatherings. There was no strict etiquette in dress (hence the blue stockings, which were frequently worn with informal attire), and no elaborate refreshments were served. Coffee, chocolate or tea with simple food were all that was offered. Conversation was the purpose of the meetings, and it was allowed to develop spontaneously with one exception — no one must ever talk politics. Card playing too, was banned; but in such brilliant company, who could wish for cards?

Certainly not Miss Alethea Newnham, who came a little diffidently to join this brilliant company under the chaperonage of Miss Hannah More. Alethea was nineteen, and it was not so very long since she had been a pupil at the excellent Seminary for young ladies kept by Miss More's sisters in Bristol.

Although she looked almost childlike in her white gown with the deep blue sash as she curtseyed shyly to the lady of the house, her intelligent grey eyes took in every detail of the much-talked-of Elizabeth Montagu's appearance. Mrs Montagu was now turned sixty, but did not look her age. She was tall and slim, with a fine-featured countenance set off by dark brown hair with no traces of grey in it, and Alethea noticed how small and white her hands were, with long tapering fingers. She greeted the young visitor graciously, taking the trouble to introduce her to several of the company who were nearest at hand.

'And Miss Burney,' said Mrs Montagu, 'you must certainly meet Miss Burney. Have you read her latest novel?'

'No, ma'am, I fear it hasn't come in my way as yet,' admitted Alethea regretfully. 'But I've read *Evelina*, and I enjoyed it very much.'

'Ah, you must certainly read *Cecilia*. You may perhaps not have much time for reading novels, when there is so much else to be read. But let me recommend you to take them with you on long coach journeys, to help while away the tedium. I always do so myself.'

Alethea agreed that this was a very good notion.

'Are you staying with Miss More?' continued her hostess.

'No, ma'am, with my aunt Mrs Manbury, in Curzon Street.'

Elizabeth Montagu nodded. 'Ah, yes, Mrs Manbury. Then you will certainly not lack for entertainment during your stay. She is one of London's most fashionable hostesses.'

Alethea smiled. 'Very true ma'am. I am quite overcome by the number of balls and parties which I'm told we are to attend, more particularly as I'm not very used to such diversions at home in Somerset.'

'But you will enjoy them all, just the same, I'm sure. I know I did so at your age.'

'I mean to enjoy everything,' replied Alethea, for the first time forgetting her awe of this great lady and allowing her natural manner to show through. 'One always welcomes experience of the world.'

'Well spoken, my dear. And if you feel that you need a change now and then from the polite chit-chat of such affairs, you must come and join our circle here. Conversation is an art, and therefore not easy to practise while dancing. Well, I must leave you now, but I will bring you to Miss Burney as soon as I can find her in all this press of people.'

She nodded graciously and passed on, leaving Alethea and Miss More with the group to whom she had introduced them. One of these people, a soberly attired gentleman in his late thirties, turned to address a few polite remarks to Alethea before finding chairs for Miss More and herself. He sat down near to them; and as Miss More soon fell into conversation with a lady on her other side, he continued to talk to Alethea.

He had a nervous manner of speech, which caused him to preface almost every remark with 'um' or 'er' and a trick of giving a little self-deprecating laugh after every statement of his opinion, as if to remove any possible offence which it might have caused. At first, she found these mannerisms so distracting that she could scarcely concentrate on what he was saying; but when she became a little more used to them, she began to enjoy his conversation.

He talked of poetry, and he talked well. Alethea, accustomed for some years to hearing the poets read aloud by her father in the evenings at home, was able to take her fair share in the conversation until mention was made of a more recent poet, Crabbe. Here she admitted her ignorance.

'Um — er — you have not read *The Village*?' asked Mr Tracy, with his nervous laugh.

Alethea shook her head. 'No, I must confess I haven't, sir. I suppose it is a pastoral poem?'

'Um — one can't truly say that he's a pastoral poet, though he certainly deals in rural subjects. But he doesn't write of Nature as Gray or Thomson do, Miss Newnham. He turns the light of reality on his subject, writing without the sentimentality which all too often pervades the work of others.' He broke off, looking earnestly at her through his myopic blue eyes. 'But you must read him and judge for yourself — um, er — yes. Perhaps you will permit me to lend you the book?'

Alethea thanked him, and he undertook to bring it round to her aunt's house for her on the following day.

'You are most kind, and I shall be very glad to borrow it,' said Alethea. 'The only thing is that I'm not perfectly certain what plans my aunt may have made for me tomorrow, so that I can't be sure of being at home to receive you.'

'Er — that doesn't matter, Miss Newnham. That is to say —' he gave an apologetic laugh — 'of course, I should be sorry to miss you and to forego the opportunity of meeting your aunt, Mrs Manbury. But I can easily leave the book, if you should not be at home.'

They had just settled this when Miss More turned towards them to join in their conversation.

'So you have been discussing poetry,' she said. 'I dare say you may not know, Alethea, that Mr Tracy himself is a poet.'

The gentleman hastily disclaimed the title. 'I am — um — the merest scribbler,' he said, in some embarrassment. 'But I am flattered that my little verses have come to your notice, ma'am.'

Shortly afterwards, the grouping in the room changed, as it was doing constantly throughout the evening, and Mr Tracy became detached from the two ladies. They passed on to a group discussing drama, and Alethea heard much praise of the superb acting of Mrs Siddons, who had recently taken the town by storm.

'Oh, how I would like to see her!' Alethea exclaimed. 'I wonder if my aunt will take me to the play while I am here?'

Miss More looked grave. 'Doubtless she will. But I am not at all sure —' She broke off for a moment, then continued in a lowered tone — 'While you were a pupil at my sister's school, you may perhaps have taken part in a performance of a play of my own called *A Search after Happiness*? In all modesty I think I may say it enjoyed some small success, in its own way.'

'Yes, ma'am, I did.'

'I was very young, of course, when I wrote that play, but I did so out of the conviction that the general run of plays acted by girls at boarding schools are not always of the purest kind, and quite unfit for females of such tender years. Since then, my dear child, the conviction has been growing upon me that play-going is not at all a proper pursuit for young people.'

'Oh, but why, ma'am? Surely there can be no harm in watching talented actors perform a work of merit? Only think what a loss to the world if no one were ever to see the works of Shakespeare performed! For I am sure you must agree that reading them is not at all the same — so much is lost which only an actor can supply.'

She spoke in a clear voice which was readily heard by the group nearest them.

'I am entirely of your opinion, ma'am,' said one gentleman, 'Plays must be acted. Reading — pshaw! Such was never the author's intention.'

This sparked off a lively discussion in which Alethea took a leading part. Miss More listened in silence, presently suggesting that they ought to be taking their leave.

'I don't know when I've had such an interesting evening!' exclaimed Alethea in the carriage on their way home. 'Certainly I enjoyed it more than anything I've attended since coming to London.'

'There are few delights equal to those of rational discourse among well-informed minds,' agreed Miss More.

Alethea laughed. 'I can scarcely claim that my mind is well-informed, ma'am. After tonight, I realise how ignorant I am on many subjects. But it was truly a stimulating experience to meet and listen to so many interesting people.'

Miss More coughed. 'I am pleased that you should have made the acquaintance of Mr Tracy. He is a gentleman of whom I am sure your parents would thoroughly approve. Besides being a man of intellect, he has a blameless character and — though one should not refine too much upon worldly considerations — he is also of good birth and fortune.'

Alethea looked a little uncomfortable at these remarks, as she could hardly fail to grasp their implications. Mr Tracy had certainly not raised any other than an intellectual interest in her; after all, he was almost twenty years her senior. She returned a slight answer to her companion, and her thoughts drifted to a conversation between herself and her elder brother Henry just before she had left home.

'So you're to go racketing in London,' he had teased her. 'I suppose you'll come back too much of the fine lady to take old Mrs Brown her broth, or teach the parish brats their letters.

That's to say if you come back at all, for no doubt you'll catch yourself a husband while you're there.'

'I'm flattered, of course, by your confidence in my talents, Harry, but I feel bound to tell you that I've never considered husband-catching among them.'

'Oh, I don't know — you're not so bad, as girls go. Besides, Mama will be disappointed in you if you fail to get yourself a man.'

'How can you say such things! I'm sure she has no such improper notion.'

He cocked a quizzical eyebrow at her. 'No? Then why do you suppose she's sending you to London? And to our Aunt Manbury, who moves in fashionable circles where eligible beaux are ten a penny?'

'Odious creature! It's no such thing! Mama says it's time I learned to mix in more varied society than can be found here in the country —'

'Exactly so, dear simpleton. And what can that possibly mean but that she plans a very different future for you than that of a country clergyman's wife?'

Alethea had dismissed the subject with a laugh, and thought no more of it until Miss More's remark brought it again to mind. She felt vaguely uneasy. Although she was nineteen, so far her thoughts had never turned towards marriage as a reality. True, marriage seemed the inevitable lot of a young woman, unless she wished to spend her whole life as a dependant in her father's household. Although she was happy enough at home for the present, she realised that some day she would wish for wider horizons, so presumably this would entail marriage. What else was there for a female to do?

No one she had so far met had given her the least inclination towards matrimony. She had not been entirely free, however, from a young girl's dreams of love, built chiefly upon what she had found in books. There seemed no connection at all between such vague dreams and the calculated husband-catching mentioned — though in a very different manner — by both her brother Henry and Miss Hannah More. Such manoeuvres seemed despicable to her. If by chance she should meet in London someone resembling her Knights of poesie, someone to arouse those feelings which at present lay dormant, then things would be different. It would be wonderful, she acknowledged; but her common sense told her that it was extremely unlikely. And if she did not meet such a person, then she would return home as she had left, an unattached girl who was quite content to be so. There could be no compromise, nothing less for her than a realisation of the dreams which she knew quite well to be wildly improbable.

Chapter III

'Well, my dear,' said Mrs Manbury to Alethea on the following morning, 'it is quite time we began to show you the Town. Now, where would you like to go first? Don't tell me, I'm sure I can hazard a guess!'

'Why, yes, ma'am, I expect you can,' replied Alethea, smiling. 'As I've never been before to London, I shall naturally wish to see the same places as every other visitor — St Paul's Cathedral, Westminster Abbey, and the like.'

Lydia had been gazing at her reflection in the mirror above the mantelshelf, but she was sufficiently diverted by this reply to turn and stare at her cousin.

'St Paul's — Westminster Abbey!' repeated Mrs Manbury in accents of surprise. 'But, my dear child, how very odd! Pray, what should you wish to see in such places?'

Alethea looked equally surprised. 'Only what everyone goes to see, I imagine — the memorials to our great writers, artists and men of action. Miss More tells me that I must be sure and see the recent memorial to David Garrick in Westminster Abbey. She is staying with Mrs Garrick at Hampton, as I believe I mentioned to you.'

'Yes, yes,' said Mrs Manbury, impatiently. 'And if Miss More chooses to escort you to the Abbey, I shall make no objection. But pray don't ask me to visit those draughty old churches, I beg! I'm sure I was never in them unless it was to some religious service or other which I was obliged to attend; and then I was sure to take a chill, for strong currents of air do not agree with my constitution. I am not delicate, precisely, but I must have warmth.'

Alethea said that she understood perfectly, and would not dream of putting her aunt to any inconvenience. 'But perhaps Lydia may like to accompany me,' she suggested.

Lydia started. 'I? Oh, dear, no, I fear it's scarcely the kind of thing I would find agreeable! Tombs and memorials are so odiously depressing to any one of a sensitive disposition. But most likely your friend Miss More will take you there, if you're really so set on it. No, I think what Mama had in mind was to take you shopping.'

'That will be very pleasant,' said Alethea, trying to look as though she meant it, 'but at present I've no need of making any purchases —'

'La, my dear, a female always has need of something or other, and it's not until one looks around the shops that one knows just what it is,' replied Mrs Manbury, with an air of profound wisdom. She moved over to the bell rope. 'Now, I'll order the carriage, and you two girls make yourselves ready as soon as may be.'

Although Alethea was a little disappointed at not being conducted on a tour of the historic sights of London, she threw herself with characteristic zest into the shopping expedition. She was used to very good shops in both Bristol and Bath, the nearest towns to her home in Somerset, but before long she had to admit that the London shopping centres eclipsed them both. In spite of what she had said, she did eventually purchase a hat in pale blue silk. It had a large brim and was ornamented with ostrich feathers.

'There, you see, my dear!' exclaimed Mrs Manbury, triumphantly. 'I told you how it would be! And I must say it becomes you extremely, besides being quite in the latest mode. For my part, I am thankful that hair is beginning to be worn dressed with less height, for I always did find those monstrous, towering erections gave me the headache, besides taking such an age to arrange. After spending almost the whole day with the hairdresser, one was so afraid of spoiling the result that it was impossible to move freely, or enter a sedan chair without taking the utmost caution. But we poor females are always called upon to suffer prodigiously in order to achieve an air of fashion, are we not?'

'Perhaps so,' replied Alethea, laughing, 'But I don't propose to suffer too acutely in the cause.'

'But you wouldn't wish to be a dowd,' objected her aunt. 'Not that you are one in the slightest — if I may say so, Alethea, I think your taste very good.'

'Thank you, ma'am,' replied Alethea, appreciating this compliment from one who was obviously a judge of such matters. 'No, I certainly wouldn't wish to be dowdy, for I do enjoy wearing pretty clothes. But there must be a limit to the rigours one's prepared to endure for vanity. Don't you agree, Lydia?'

Lydia assented without much conviction, as her attention had been claimed by a bonnet trimmed with coquelicot ribbons which she was thinking of purchasing. After trying on several others she found herself quite unable to decide upon any single one, so ended by taking three. The smiling milliner did not trust any of her minions to show the ladies out, but herself accompanied them to the door, bowing profoundly as an indication of her great pleasure in their visit.

'Well, girls,' said Mrs Manbury as they made their way to the carriage. 'I hope you're satisfied, for I am so fatigued I declare I could not step into another shop this day if my wardrobe depended on it! And no wonder, for it's past three o'clock already. We must go home this minute — we are to visit Vauxhall this evening, recollect, so there's little enough time to dine and make ourselves ready. I mean to take a rest in my boudoir before I attempt anything more, and if you take my advice, you'll do likewise. I must warn you that there's nothing like fatigue for bringing on wrinkles and crows feet.'

The two girls exchanged pitying glances at this remark, for the first time feeling some affinity for each other. They refused to be daunted by such bogies at their age.

They had almost reached their carriage when Lydia noticed two gentlemen who were approaching among the strollers on the pavement. She pinched her mother's arm, making Mrs Manbury start.

'Mama, look!' she whispered in an aside that only just reached Alethea's ear. 'Beau Devenish and Lord Calver — they haven't seen us yet. Don't walk on too fast, or they won't catch up with us before we reach the carriage.'

Mrs Manbury had begun to step out more briskly with the carriage in sight, but now she obediently slackened her pace. Lydia turned to her cousin and began an animated conversation designed to give any onlooker the impression that she was quite oblivious of the passers-by. Alethea good naturedly played up to her cousin, but she was hard put to it not to burst out laughing. She wondered if Lydia always conducted this kind of charade whenever she encountered gentlemen of her acquaintance in the street, or if this was a special performance for the exclusive benefit of this particular pair. She remembered having heard Devenish's name mentioned previously by both her aunt and cousin. She had paid little heed at the time, because there is rarely much interest in gossip about people whom one does not know; but now Lydia's antics had aroused her curiosity. She took the opportunity, therefore, of scrutinising the two gentlemen carefully when presently they halted to speak to Mrs Manbury and her daughter. It was easy for her to concentrate on studying them, as she had little part to play in the conversation after being formally introduced.

Both men were in their late twenties and dressed in the height of fashion. Lord Calver, in a well fitting brown coat, was slightly the shorter of the two, with a square, good humoured face and a ready laugh that never seemed forced. His companion's coat was blue but Alethea's eye was irresistibly drawn to his waistcoat. It was quite unlike anything she had seen in Somerset even though her brother Henry, now in his second year at Oxford, did set up to be a bit of a dandy. It was square cut, shorter than the more usual style, and patterned in stripes of white and pale blue.

When she finally removed her gaze from this garment to its owner's face, she surprised an ironical twinkle in his eye. She coloured and looked hastily away, realising that she had been caught looking him over. But in a few moments all his attention was again on Lydia, to whom he was chatting in a languid manner very different from Lord Calver's animation. Alethea ventured to continue her scrutiny. Haughty, she decided — yes, that was the word for his expression.

A long, thin countenance with a classical nose, finely arched brows and a pair of mocking hazel eyes. Not always mocking, either, she amended, as for a moment she caught a flash of some more disturbing emotion when his gaze dwelt on Lydia's charming face. She did not feel disposed to like him very much.

The conversation was only desultory and soon came to an end. The gentlemen handed the ladies into their carriage, then stood for a moment watching it move along into the press of traffic before they resumed their stroll.

'A winsome girl, Miss Manbury,' remarked Lord Calver, 'But I think you don't need me to tell you that,' he added, with a grin. 'What think you of the little cousin?'

Devenish grimaced. 'Pretty enough, but not in my style, Will. I fancy that shrewd eye of hers don't miss much, and I prefer my females to be beautiful and witless — a more comfortable arrangement, you'll agree.'

'Miss Manbury is not precisely witless,' objected his companion.

'As near as makes no matter,' said Beau Devenish, with a shrug.

'Devil take it, James, you're an odd fellow! I thought you admired her — you're always dancing attendance on her.'

'Lud, yes, but what has that to say to anything? Besides, my dear chap, next month I may think otherwise — who can tell? It's lamentable,' he added, with a yawn, 'but one is so demmed fickle.'

'You most certainly are, old fellow. You're a cold fish — can none of them touch your heart, I wonder?'

Devenish raised a quizzical eyebrow. 'My heart, did you say? That organ which, according to the findings of one Dr Harvey, is primarily responsible for circulating the blood? In that sense I grant its importance, but in any other, I refuse to allow it to dominate my conduct.'

'Ah, well, it takes all sorts to make a world,' laughed Calver. 'For my part, I'm not at all of your mind. My father tells me it's high time I settled down and produced an heir, and I dare say the old man's in the right of it, so I'm looking about me for some eligible female who ain't too plain, and then I shall make her a present of my hand and heart, too — that's if she'll have 'em.'

'A capital scheme,' said Devenish, drily. 'And I fancy you've already got someone in mind, by all the signs.'

'How d'you know?' demanded Calver, reddening, 'Devil a word have I said to anyone!'

Devenish looked at him pityingly. 'My dear chap, haven't you heard that actions speak louder than words? But never fear, a certain young lady's name shall never cross my lips. You must tell me,' he added, with a slightly curling lip, 'When I may wish you joy.'

Meanwhile, the gentlemen themselves were under discussion in the Manbury's town coach.

'Of the two, I declare I could almost prefer Calver,' remarked Mrs Manbury, heaving a heartfelt sigh at the luxury of taking the weight off her feet. 'He has not quite the dash of Devenish, of course —'

'Oh, no! But then,' said Lydia, 'they do not call Sir James Devenish "the Beau" for nothing.'

'The Beau? Do they so?' asked Alethea. 'You do mean the one with the arrogant countenance, I suppose? Introductions are always so confusing, but I believe I have it right,' she added.

'Well, yes, I suppose you might say there was a trifle of height in his manner,' allowed Mrs Manbury, judicially, 'But, of course, taking into account his birth and fortune, that's only to be expected. He's known everywhere as Beau Devenish, for besides that he is a prodigiously handsome man, he's always dressed in the first style of fashion.'

'That would account for the striped waistcoat,' said Alethea. 'I've seen nothing like it in Somerset, but perhaps it's quite usual in London?'

'Usual?' repeated Lydia, in mock horror. 'He would hate to hear you say so! Beau Devenish sets the style, not follows it. I dare say every gentleman will be copying it before the month's out, and then he'll grow tired of it and start something quite different.'

'Truly?' There was contempt in Alethea's tone. 'To be in the fashion is one thing, but to be so over-concerned with such a trivial subject surely argues a trivial mind? Neither would I say, myself, that he is handsome. Certainly he has good features and rather fine eyes; but his expression is such that it robs his countenance of any charm it might otherwise possess.'

'Hoity toity!' exclaimed Lydia slightly offended. 'Now who is arrogant, pray? It's plain to see, cousin, as far as you're concerned that Beau Devenish failed to make the impression he generally does on our sex! Not that he'll care for that, I promise you — I dare say he didn't so much as notice you.'

Mrs Manbury felt bound to soften this comment. 'Well, if he did not, Lydia, it was only because he has eyes for no one but you at present. I noticed that Calver glanced more than once at Alethea, and I must say she looks very becomingly in that blue gown.'

'It is kind in you to say so, Aunt. Fortunately my whole happiness doesn't depend upon being noticed by chance acquaintances. But am I to understand that Sir James Devenish and Lydia —?'

'Oh, no,' cut in Mrs Manbury, hurriedly, 'you are not to be supposing that there is anything serious! The truth is, he's a shocking flirt, and any girl who's such a goose as to take his attentions seriously has only herself to thank if she gets hurt. Lydia has more sense than that, haven't you, my love?'

'You know very well that I have, Mama,' replied Lydia, calmly.

'He takes up with first one girl and then another in the most shameless way,' continued Mrs Manbury. 'But everyone knows by now that he means nothing by it — the most determined match-making Mamas have quite given up all hope of him!'

'I see,' said Alethea, thoughtfully. 'It's to be hoped that at some time or other he doesn't find himself hoist with his own petard.'

'Are you supposing you might be the one to do it, cousin?' asked Lydia, with a hint of malice. 'I dislike to disappoint you, but I must tell you that I don't think you're quite in Beau Devenish's style.'

'And I'm perfectly certain that he's not in mine, so we are very well quit of each other,' laughed Alethea. 'I'm looking forward to visiting Vauxhall,' she went on, thinking a change of subject might be a good idea. 'My brothers have been there, and they say there's a spectacle in the gardens that I must be sure not to miss — but they won't tell me what it is, in that teasing way brothers have. Pray, Aunt, do enlighten me!'

'Well, since you're to see it for yourself in so short a while, we may as well keep up the mystery for a little longer, don't you think, Lydia?' asked Mrs Manbury, smiling.

Lydia shrugged. 'Just as you wish, but it's no great matter, after all. Who is in our party, Mama? Have you asked anyone besides Caroline and Fothergill?'

'Why, no. I thought we would make it quite a small family party on this occasion. I can't ask Eleanor, of course, as she is increasing and the excitement would be bad for her, so I'm afraid,' turning to Alethea, 'you'll have to wait for another occasion to meet Lydia's eldest sister and her husband, Sir Roger Middleham.'

Alethea made some civil reply, but Lydia cut into it.

'Then we're to have only Papa and George to escort us?' she asked, pettishly. 'Upon my word, it will be a dull party! Four females to two men, and both of them related to us!'

'We shall meet with plenty of our acquaintances there I dare say,' said her mother, soothingly. 'One sees all the world at Vauxhall, you know.'

Chapter IV

The party that set out for Vauxhall that evening included Lydia's father, as well as her elder sister Caroline, and Caroline's husband, Lord Fothergill. The latter part of the journey was made by water, passing the Archbishop's palace at Lambeth on the way. It was dusk and the last red streaks of the setting sun still lingered in the sky. Lights were springing up along the banks of the Thames; the lamps of the pleasure boats made golden ripples across the dark water. Always alive to atmosphere, Alethea sighed with deep content, and told Lydia that the scene put her in mind of some lines of Milton's *Paradise Lost*. At home, a remark, such as this would have seemed normal enough; but both Mrs Manbury and Lord Fothergill stared at the speaker.

'Oh, pooh, poetry!' said Lydia, in a contemptuous tone.

Alethea subsided with a sigh, retreating into her own thoughts, which echoed the calm beauty of the scene before her.

Her first view of the gardens continued the enchantment. The pleasant, tree-lined walks were hung with coloured lanterns; sweet strains of music drifted through the air of what was an unusually balmy May evening. Moving among crowds of gaily dressed people, the Manburys made their way to the source of the music, a handsomely decorated stage set amid trees heavy with cherry blossom. Here Mr Manbury guided them to one of the ground floor supper boxes, where they would be able both to hear the concert and watch the passers-by.

He paused briefly on the way to sketch a bow before a box occupied by a lady and three gentlemen. One of these was a lumpy, unkempt creature in a baggy coat and a bushy wig that was badly singed in front.

'That,' whispered Mrs Manbury to Alethea, 'is Dr Johnson, my dear. Did ever you see such a fright? But one cannot altogether ignore him.'

'Ignore the compiler of the Dictionary? I should think not,' replied Alethea, indignantly. 'It will be a sad day when we choose to overlook one of the country's foremost scholars.'

'Oh, to be sure — but such an odd looking creature, you must own.'

Alethea might have replied to this, but just then they arrived at their own box and were busy settling themselves into chairs.

'Mama, I believe that's the Prince of Wales,' said Caroline Fothergill, craning over the parapet of the box.

'Where?' asked Mrs Manbury, following suit. 'Oh, yes, I see — with the female in the green and white striped gown, standing under that tree. Alethea, do but come here a moment.'

Alethea obeyed, and was just in time to see the Prince disappear into the crowd with one arm fondly encircling the lady in the striped gown.

'Now, I wonder who she can be?' mused Mrs Manbury. 'He's finished with Perdita Robinson, but I haven't yet heard his name coupled with anyone else's. What do you think, Caro?'

She turned away to consult with her daughter, but Alethea remained leaning over the box, studying the crowd. A passing buck ogled her, and she drew back hastily. Her uncle raised his quizzing glass, quickly sending the offender about his business.

'If you are not to expose yourselves to impertinent stares,' said Mr Manbury, severely, 'I advise you to keep your heads within the shelter of the box. There is always a smattering of riff-raff at such places as these.'

The ladies obediently sat down again, contenting themselves for the moment with what could be readily seen from their vantage point. There was plenty to interest and amuse them in the passing crowd, composed of people from all walks of life. The fashionable rubbed shoulders with more ordinary folk whom Mr Manbury referred to contemptuously as 'Cits', while here and there could be seen the painted faces of females who came yet lower in the social scale. Alethea soon gave up all attempts to pay close attention to the concert which continued as a pleasing background to the chatter and movement of the crowd. Only when a favourite singer was performing would the noise abate a little.

When the concert came to an end, supper was served. This was a cold collation of ham, chicken and beef, with fruit tarts, cheesecakes, syllabubs laced with wine and fresh fruit.

'Let me recommend you to try the special Vauxhall Nectar,' suggested Mr Manbury to Alethea, offering her a small glass. 'An evening at the Gardens is not complete without it.'

'What is it, sir?' she asked, taking up the glass and sipping cautiously at its contents.

'It's a mixture of rum and syrup with some herbs added,' he replied. 'But I must warn you, my dear, that it's more potent than you might suppose.'

Alethea, who had never before tasted rum and did not care very much for her experience of it, took one more sip before setting down the glass and saying diffidently that she thought perhaps she would prefer some lemonade. She hoped this would not give offence to her uncle; but she need not have worried, for he only laughed, saying that it was not in general a favourite beverage with females.

'You're quite wrong, Papa, for I like it of all things!' exclaimed Caroline Fothergill, draining her glass and passing it over to be refilled. 'But I can't bear that odious Arrack punch which they give one here.'

'Demmit, Caro, I should think not,' remarked her husband, reproachfully. 'Punch ain't a proper drink for females, mean to say.'

She threw him a glance of withering scorn. 'Oh, if one is only to do what is proper!'

Alethea had been studying the pair covertly from time to time, and had come to the conclusion that no one could possibly think them a happily married couple.

Caroline was not unlike her sister Lydia in looks. She had the same round, dimpled face with a creamy skin and masses of soft, dark hair; but when she was not laughing, her mouth set too often into discontented lines, and her eyes lacked the vivacity of Lydia's. Her husband, was a rabbity-faced man in his early thirties. His dress was fashionable to the point of dandyism, but the air of distinction which had been so marked in both Beau Devenish and Lord Calver was somehow lacking. Alethea, who always derived a quiet pleasure from studying her fellow creatures, decided that this was partly due to a lack of intelligence in his expression. He spoke seldom, and when he did it was always of trivialities. His wife treated him with barely concealed contempt, and never addressed him unless it was to say something disagreeable.

Once supper was over, Caroline became restless. 'Why don't we walk about a little?' she demanded. 'I declare I'm tired of sitting still! We're almost sure to meet someone interesting among all these people — besides, there are to be fireworks later on, and one wants to secure a good place, not too far back in the crowd.'

'Oh, my dear, I couldn't walk another step!' exclaimed her mother, pushing back her chair from the table and sliding down into a more relaxed attitude. 'But I dare say Fothergill will accompany you and the girls, if you wish to go, won't you, George? Then Papa and I will just rest here for a while. Fireworks are no great matter at our time of life, you know.'

'Greatest pleasure in the world,' replied Fothergill, affably. 'Miss Newnham may like to see the Waterfall, too. Plenty of time to go there first, before taking up places for the firework display.'

Accordingly they left the box to join the constant stream of passing people.

'Regret I haven't three arms,' said Fothergill, with one of his inane laughs. 'Shall I take you, Caro, my dear, or one of the others? Wouldn't do for one of you to be walking on her own in this crush.'

'Oh, take our cousin!' snapped Caroline, catching Lydia's arm. 'Lydia and I haven't had a gossip together for an age. Anyway, it's a slow thing to be walking with one's husband, and not at all the fashion.'

'As you say, m'dear,' he answered mildly, offering Alethea his arm.

As they strolled along in pairs keeping close together, Alethea did her best to maintain a conversation with her companion, but soon found that he had nothing to volunteer and little to reply to her remarks. Lydia and her sister, on the other hand, were chatting away at a great rate. Presently they heard a rumbling like that of thunder ahead of them. Alethea looked in the direction of the noise and saw that it came from a huge waterfall cascading over a high rock.

'Mind your purses! Mind your purses!' These warning shouts came from some of the Garden's custodians.

'Pickpockets?' queried Alethea, as they pressed closer to the Waterfall.

'Plenty of 'em about everywhere,' assented Fothergill. 'But worse where the crowd's thick, like this.'

Alethea took a firmer grip on her reticule, although there was little in it of value at present. She gazed wonderingly at the sheet of water which was falling from a great height in such a remarkably regular flow.

'But surely it's *not* a genuine waterfall!' she exclaimed after watching for a moment. 'It's an enormous painting of one, and the cloth is being agitated in such a way that it stimulates an actual fall of water! The sound, too — that's manufactured by some machinery. How very ingenious!'

'Quite right,' agreed Fothergill. 'Very sharp of you, ma'am, to spot it so quickly. It takes people in for quite a time, as a rule.'

'Well, now I know why Henry — that's one of my brothers, you know — wouldn't describe the Spectacle to me. He said he didn't wish to spoil my enjoyment of it.'

They stood looking at it for a little while, then by common consent made their way to that part of the Gardens where the firework display was to take place. Here some benches were set out which were already well filled. They all began to look about them to try and find four vacant seats. Suddenly Lydia gave a start and nudged her sister.

'Look over there!' she exclaimed. 'No, there, stupid! Over to our left. Do you see who it is?'

The other obediently followed her gaze and saw that it was directed at a group of three gentlemen, each with his arm entwined about the waist of a personable young female.

'Devenish, Horam and Calver,' pronounced Caroline in instant recognition. 'As for the females, some ladybirds or other, I don't doubt.'

'No, really, m'dear,' protested her husband, with an uneasy glance at Lydia and Alethea.

'Don't be so odiously stuffy, George! Lydia knows well enough what a ladybird is, and as for Alethea — well, girls are not near so innocent as they would have the men think, I assure you! She really is prodigiously attractive, don't you think?' she went on, staring at the girl in Beau Devenish's embrace. 'Who is she, George? Do you know?'

He coughed. 'Rather fancy — name of Travers, Kitty Travers, an Opera dancer,' he mumbled. 'Much sought after — hm! — by all accounts.' He looked uneasily at his wife, then touched her on the arm. 'Four seats over there, m'dear. Shall we take them?'

They allowed themselves to be settled on the bench, but Lydia's eyes were still on the amorous couple, who had not yet sat down.

'What's amiss, Lydia?' Caroline sounded amused. 'Don't you care to see your gallant cavorting with someone else? The more fool you, my dear — you know his reputation well enough.'

'It's not that,' replied Lydia, in an angry tone. 'But to be in such company and — and so shamelessly familiar in public —'

'Stuff! A Vauxhall romp — I'll wager George here has taken part in many a one, haven't you, George?'

Fothergill looked taken aback, and stammered that he had put by such diversions on his marriage.

Caroline shrugged. 'Much I care if you have not,' she said, in a tone of indifference. 'A female's nothing but a fool if she expects men to be other than they are. Cheer up, Lydia, Devenish will wait on you tomorrow with flowers, and be as attentive as ever, I'll be bound.'

'Then he can spare himself the trouble, for I'll not receive him!' snapped Lydia. 'And I do think, Caroline, that you have by far too free a way of talking — you will give our cousin a disgust of you.'

Fothergill, greatly daring, was about to concur with this view, but Alethea diplomatically broke in to say that she thought the fireworks were about to start, as she had seen some officials appear on the platform. The others stopped talking at once, and in a few minutes the first rockets soared skywards, leaving a trail of brightly coloured stars.

Chapter V

The ladies put in a late appearance at breakfast on the following morning, and it soon became evident that Lydia, at any rate, was sadly out of humour.

'I thought perhaps we might make a few calls this morning,' said Mrs Manbury, as she rose from the table. 'Of course, I shall arrange a ball for Alethea in a week or two, when she may meet everyone. But it can scarcely be thought pleasant to encounter a room full of strangers, so in the meantime we must introduce her to some of our oldest friends.'

Alethea thanked her aunt feelingly for this, but Lydia pulled a face.

'That's all very well, Mama, but need we start today? I am not at all in the mood for visiting. Where did you mean to go?'

'Well, certainly to the Allertons. And they are such very old friends that you cannot possibly object to paying a short call on them, Lydia. Why, you practically grew up with Felicia and Clarinda, and I'm sure they are the most amiable girls in the world, and always delighted to see you.'

'Oh, yes, they are amiable enough, like all the Allertons,' answered Lydia, pettishly, 'But I am too odiously fatigued this morning for polite chit-chat. I would far rather stay at home.'

Mrs Manbury was a reasonably indulgent mother in matters which she judged unimportant, but she was inflexible when she had decided on a certain course.

'Very well,' she said, compressing her lips. 'Alethea and I will go alone. And I trust we may find you in a better humour on our return.'

Lydia made no reply to this, but yawned ostentatiously.

'The child is a trifle fagged,' allowed Mrs Manbury as they settled themselves in the smart town carriage. 'It's scarce to be wondered at after so much activity yesterday. I must confess to feeling a trifle done-up myself, but I am determined to exert myself for your sake.'

Alethea did not believe that fatigue was the real cause of her cousin's irritability, but she kept the thought to herself as she thanked her aunt.

'You will like the Allertons,' went on Mrs Manbury. 'We have known them all our lives. They are a large family, mostly girls. Some are married and settled in establishments of their own, and some are away at school. There are two girls at home who have been out a year or so, but up to now there's been no serious sign of either making a match. Felicia is the elder — she's one and twenty — and the more elegant of the two. Poor Clarinda is rather plump, but as good-natured a girl as ever breathed. She's the same age as you, nineteen. The eldest son, Vivyan, is a pleasant, agreeable young man, too, though you won't be seeing him, as he doesn't live at home. One wonders that he's not yet married, for he's turned seven and twenty; but I fancy myself that he's more than a trifle smitten with Lydia. However, that could not come to anything. Lydia has other aspirations. He is one of Beau Devenish's set,' she added.

That man again, thought Alethea. He seemed to have a way of creeping into the Manburys' conversation. Perhaps, in spite of all they said about not taking his attentions to Lydia seriously, they were secretly nourishing a hope that this time he might mean matrimony. Could this be what her aunt meant by Lydia's aspirations? However that might be, Alethea saw no signs of love in her cousin. If Lydia did wish to marry Sir James Devenish, it was for more worldly reasons.

It was only a short distance to the Allertons' house in South Audley Street. Mrs Allerton was at home, the butler told them, and would be happy to receive Mrs Manbury and her niece. They were shown into a comfortable parlour on the ground floor, and Mrs Allerton, a plump, fair woman with an amiable countenance, came forward to greet them.

'Olivia, my dear, how very nice to see you!' She kissed Mrs Manbury affectionately. 'And this is your sister's daughter? Clarinda, love, this is Miss Alethea Newnham, who's staying with Mrs Manbury for a while. You must become better acquainted.'

Clarinda, a pink and white blonde who was decidedly well covered, came forward to take Alethea's hand and make her welcome. Alethea glanced towards the window; a boy of about fifteen had been sitting there reading a book when they entered. Now he rose, hastily putting the volume aside and looking round him like a cornered animal. Mrs Allerton turned towards him.

'Simon, my love, come and make your bow to the ladies. He's had the measles, you know,' she explained to Mrs Manbury, 'and once he was out of infection, they sent him home to recuperate for a week or two. He's such a dreamer, and always has his nose in a book,' she added fondly, oblivious of the quick flush that showed in her offspring's otherwise pale cheeks. 'I keep telling him it would do him far more good to take a walk in the Park. I think I shall pack him off to my sister at Weymouth — the sea air will soon pull him up again, don't you agree?'

Simon had obediently approached, making an awkward bow and speaking some words of greeting in a barely audible voice.

'What are you reading?' Alethea asked him with an encouraging smile.

The ebbing flush returned to his cheeks at being directly addressed. 'Oh, nothing much,' he mumbled. 'It's — that's to say — it's poetry.'

Obviously conversation with adults was a torment to him, and if the others had been listening, Alethea would have let this remark go; but Clarinda had turned away to ring the bell for some refreshment, and the two older ladies were absorbed in their own conversation.

'I'm very fond of poetry myself,' she said. 'May I see your book?'

'Of — of course, ma'am.'

He turned to fetch it and Alethea, following close behind, was able to take it from his nerveless grasp before it fell to the floor.

'Oh, Gray's *Elegy*,' she said. 'I know it well, and love it. Pray, what do you think of it?'

'As to that, ma'am,' he replied, shakily, 'I fear my opinion can scarce be of any interest to you — I'm not in any way qualified to judge —'

'But of course you are! Every reader is entitled to an opinion, whether he be scholar or student. Don't you agree?'

The genuine interest in her voice and the kindliness of her quiet grey eyes steadied him a little.

'Entitled — yes, I suppose so,' he said, with more confidence. 'But whether that makes his opinion any more *interesting*, I would take leave to doubt, ma'am.'

She laughed. 'Well, you have the best of that argument! Tell me, do you read much poetry?'

He nodded. 'Yes, and —' he paused, looking furtively round at his family — 'I beg you won't mention this, Miss Newnham, but I try to write it, too.'

'Do you? I used to try when I was younger, but I fear I never succeeded in producing anything other than very bad verse, so I decided for the sake of mankind in general to give it up,' said Alethea, with a laugh.

'I dare say no one minded that you should write poetry,' he said wistfully. 'As you're a female, I mean.'

'What should it matter which sex one is, in that regard?' asked Alethea, in surprise.

'A good deal, I may tell you, ma'am. If I were to let them know I do it, they would think me a rare namby-pamby!'

'You mean the other boys at school?' He nodded. 'Well, that may be, at present,' said Alethea encouragingly, 'but soon you will be at the University, and then you may write what you choose. Meanwhile, I will keep your secret, and you mustn't betray mine. For,' she added, with one of her most charming smiles, 'no one wishes to be known as a *failed* poet, female or not.'

His answering grin told her that he felt quite at his ease again.

'Simon, my love, what can you be thinking of?' demanded his mother, suddenly looking up from her conversation. 'Aren't you going to offer Miss Newnham a chair? You mustn't bore her with talk of your books, you know.'

This had the effect of making him colour up again. He mumbled an apology, set a chair for Alethea and retreated to his window seat. Clarinda now claimed Alethea's attention, and presently Simon made some excuse and went out of the room, leaving Alethea to reflect how clumsy the most loving of mothers can be at times.

'Poor darling, I fear we've frightened him off,' laughed Mrs Allerton. 'But it's too much to expect a boy to remain closeted in a room full of female company! Why did not Lydia come with you, Olivia? The girls are always pleased to see her here. I trust she isn't indisposed?'

'Oh, nothing but the headache. We were at Vauxhall yesterday evening, and I think we were all feeling a trifle jaded. She sent her apologies, and was sure you'd understand.'

'Oh, these young people lead a very rackety existence, to be sure,' agreed her friend. 'It's a wonder to me that they can keep it up and still retain their looks — but there, we were just as bad when we were young! Felicia, by the way, is with the dressmaker at present, but she should be finished presently, and then she will join us. And that reminds me, you may see Vivyan, too, for he said he would be calling on us some time this morning. He has something to discuss with his father — but I fancy it concerns horses, not marriage,' she added laughing. 'I have quite given up hope in that direction, though with so many lovely girls in Town every season, one feels the young men must be harder to please than when we were young. There is Devenish, too, and his friends Calver and Horam, to name only a few who are well into their twenties and still in the bachelor state. I don't know what the world's coming to, I'm sure.'

The refreshments arrived and were handed round. Alethea, deprived of what had promised to be quite an interesting conversation with young Simon, settled down to talk to Clarinda Allerton. It did not take long to discover that she had very different interests from those of her younger brother. She prattled away gaily on topics such as social events, fashion, her family and friends, as though these were the mainspring of her life. Alethea was not surprised to hear her say with evident sincerity that Lydia was one of her dearest friends. Clarinda Allerton, like her Mama, was clearly a warm-hearted, uncritical girl ready to believe the best of everybody. Indeed, it was doubtful if she had the wit to see beyond what appeared on the surface.

For a moment, the more perceptive Alethea almost envied Clarinda. It must be so much more comfortable, she reflected, to be possessed of this easy temperament than of her own analytical, questioning cast of mind. Almost as a matter of habit, she was for ever studying people; she could never help noticing the word or action that betrayed a hidden motive or emotion. Sometimes, of course, she would be mistaken; but too often people unwittingly revealed themselves to her, giving her either amusement or pain. It was fortunate that the strong sense of humour she had inherited from her father usually enabled her to keep a sense of proportion about these revelations, otherwise she might have been in some danger of taking herself too seriously.

Chapter VI

They had been sitting for some time with the Allertons and were thinking of taking their leave when Felicia Allerton, accompanied by two gentlemen, burst into the room.

'Mama,' she began, 'here's Viv come to see us, and he's brought Sir James with him — oh, I beg your pardon I didn't realise you had company.'

She came over to Mrs Manbury with hand outstretched. 'How do you do, ma'am? Is not Lydia with you?'

Mrs Manbury offered her cheek to be kissed and explained about Lydia, afterwards introducing Alethea. Felicia Allerton was taller and more slender than her sister, with the same blonde hair and fair complexion. She was wearing a very pretty yellow gown with a white sash, which gave her a fresh, Spring-like look. Her brother Vivyan, who was dressed for riding, had the same colouring as his sisters and looked, thought Alethea as she made her curtsy, a very pleasant young man.

Beau Devenish looked as immaculate as ever as he watched the introductions with a faintly cynical eye, before bowing to the ladies and apologising in his languid way for coming straight from the stables to Mrs Allerton's parlour.

'Yes, we're sorry to burst in upon you like this, Mama, but we thought you'd be alone. Anyway, Devenish and I have come to see father about that horse he wanted, so we'll remove ourselves at once, and leave you in peace.'

'Oh, no, pray do stay and talk to us for just a few moments!' pleaded Mrs Allerton — 'I see you so seldom, though I don't know quite how that is!' She turned to Devenish. 'You'll take a glass of wine, Sir James? Ring the bell, Vivyan — there's nothing here suitable for gentlemen.'

The two men allowed themselves to be persuaded, Vivyan sitting down on the sofa between Mrs Manbury and his mother, while Devenish, having first placed a chair for Felicia, took a seat close to the three girls. Felicia, who seemed to be something of a rattle, was soon talking away at a great rate to Devenish, who answered her in the same drawling, slightly bored tone that Alethea had noticed at her first meeting with him. Clarinda, obviously a little in awe of such a noted Beau, contented herself with an occasional comment whenever it was called for by her sister, otherwise keeping up a desultory conversation with Alethea.

Presently Alethea found herself being addressed by Devenish. 'And how do you like London, Miss Newnham?' he asked.

'I scarce know, sir. I haven't seen much of the town as yet.'

'I suppose not. Still it's a question that one must ask, you know,' he drawled.

'Even if one is tolerably certain of the answer?' she parried, her eyes twinkling.

'To be sure. Most of our conversation consists of questions to which we know the answers. Don't you agree, ma'am?'

'I think it depends,' she said, judicially, 'what exactly one means by conversation.'

'And what exactly do you mean by it, Miss Newnham?' he asked, with a languid smile.

'You mean to quiz me, sir, but I shall not play,' she said, in mock severity.

'Not at all — I am in deadly earnest. This is one question to which I cannot anticipate an answer.'

She looked incredulous. 'I can't believe that. I think my meaning was clear enough.'

'And so do I,' put in Felicia, not wishing to be excluded. 'You meant that there is polite conversation, where everyone says what is expected, and — and the other kind.'

'Where everyone says what is not expected, I collect?' asked Devenish, his smile widening.

'Oh, you are quizzing *me* now, Sir James, and it's too bad of you! But you know very well what I'm trying to say — besides polite talk, one can have friendly, informal conversations, or — or serious ones, such as my brother Simon delights in.'

'Your brother started a most interesting conversation with me when Aunt Olivia and I first arrived,' remarked Alethea. 'Unfortunately, it was interrupted.'

'May one be permitted to ask the subject?' drawled Devenish.

'Oh, of course, for it was nothing of a private nature. We were speaking of poetry.'

Devenish nodded mockingly. 'Poetry — I see. Do you read much in that way, ma'am?'

'Not near as much as I should like,' replied Alethea somewhat nettled by his tone. 'But there are so many books one wishes to read.'

'Oh, if you talked of books to Simon, he will like you prodigiously!' said Felicia. 'I fear Clarinda and I are not at all bookish. Neither is Viv — though I don't think any the worse of him for that,' she added, with an affectionate glance at her brother. 'But Simon's the clever one of the family. As Papa says, he'll be far better suited to Oxford than my brother Jack, who is for ever in some kind of scrape or another.'

Devenish now looked distinctly bored. He turned to Alethea again.

'I see Miss Manbury is not with you.'

'No. We were all at Vauxhall yesterday evening, and Lydia felt too fatigued to come out with us.'

'Vauxhall? I trust you found it tolerably amusing?'

Alethea was not normally a touchy girl, but she found herself becoming increasingly irritated by Beau Devenish's manner. She told herself fair-mindedly that no doubt it was natural to him, and he could no more help it than another man — Mr Tracy, for instance — could help a stammer, or possibly a harsh voice. But the fact remained that his habitual air of indifference, amounting at times to boredom, and the supercilious tone which his drawling voice managed to impart to all his remarks, did arouse a certain animosity in her. She could not resist the impulse to try and shake him out of his detachment.

'Prodigiously,' she replied. 'Oh, by the way, we caught sight of you in the distance, Sir James, while we were there. You were with a party of friends at the place where the firework display was held. We were looking for seats at the time, and so, I believe, were you.'

'Indeed?' If anything, the drawl was more pronounced, but there was no sign that Alethea's shaft had gone home. 'I am very sorry that we should not have encountered your party during the course of the evening. But at least you can say now that you've seen something of London, ma'am.'

'I suppose I can,' replied Alethea, abandoning for the moment her attempt to rouse him from his habitual languor. 'I certainly found it a most entertaining visit. But I still haven't seen any of the places I was most looking forward to visiting when I came here.'

'May I ask which places you mean?'

'Oh, Westminster Abbey, St Paul's Cathedral, and the like.'

He raised an eyebrow. 'So that was what you most hoped to do here? Well, ma'am, I imagine there is still time enough.'

Alethea agreed dubiously.

'You seem uncertain, Miss Newnham. Perhaps you are soon to leave London?'

'Oh, no, I am fixed here for a month or so — that is, if it should suit my Aunt's convenience. But Mrs Manbury and Lydia tell me that they are not at all disposed to go to such places,' she added, with a guilty glance in Mrs Manbury's direction, 'and I don't well know how it can be managed otherwise. However,' she went on, with more energy, 'I dare say I shall hit on some scheme.'

'Oh, what a pity!' exclaimed Clarinda. 'But I will gladly go with you, Miss Newnham, rather than you should be disappointed.' This was generous, for she herself had no interest whatever in historic buildings. 'I wonder if we could persuade Viv to escort us?'

Hearing the last part of this speech, Allerton looked up from his conversation with the two older ladies. 'You wonder if I would escort you where, Clarry?' he asked, suspiciously. 'Let me tell you I don't aim to squire my sisters around Town — plenty of other men in line for that kind of thing, surely?'

'You are very good, Miss Allerton,' put in Alethea, hastily, 'but of course I could not dream of putting you or your brother to so much trouble on my account.'

'There, Allerton,' said Devenish, laughing softly. 'You can't leave it at that — you can't possibly disoblige a lady. What do you say if we make up a party to visit London's historic buildings? I dare say most of us have never set foot in them, unless in the course of duty.'

'Visit historic buildings?' repeated Allerton, aghast. 'Whoever thought of a deuced odd notion like that? I must say, Devenish, it don't sound like you!'

'You are quite right. It was Miss Newnham's notion. It seems she came to Town with the firm intention of seeing St Paul's Cathedral and Westminster Abbey. She's quite set her heart on it.'

He regarded his friend with a gleam of mischief in his eye.

'Oh — oh, well, in that case,' stuttered Allerton, returning this look with one which promised a reckoning later. 'I beg your pardon, ma'am — of course, I'll be happy to oblige. A party, you say, Devenish? My sisters, I suppose —' he glanced at them a trifle unlovingly — 'and Miss Newnham of course. Do I understand that you mean to go yourself?' Devenish nodded, smiling cynically. 'Yes, well, it could be managed, certainly. I don't suppose,' Allerton added, brightening, and turning to address Mrs Manbury, 'that Lydia might possibly feel inclined to make one of the party?'

Mrs Manbury looked doubtful. 'Oh, dear, I really cannot say. It's not at all the kind of thing she cares for in general — indeed, we did tell Alethea so from the first — but if you are all to go together —'

'I'm sure she would allow herself to be persuaded, ma'am,' put in Clarinda. 'Dear Lydia is so very good natured.'

Alethea happened to glance at Devenish at that moment, and saw the familiar cynical gleam in his eye. She looked away again hastily, for fear of breaking into a laugh.

'Yes, to be sure,' agreed Allerton, who evidently found it easier than Devenish to believe in Miss Manbury's good nature. 'And with a party, it will not be so bad — that is to say,' he amended hastily, 'we should all enjoy the outing. I'm not sure that it may not turn out to be a capital notion,' he continued, warming to his theme. 'Now, when will it suit you to go? No time like the present — how about tomorrow?'

This led to a somewhat tedious review of everyone's engagements, but in the end it was settled that tomorrow would suit all those present.

'As for Lydia,' remarked Mrs Manbury, 'I really cannot promise for her. I must speak to her first. I know of no previous engagement, but there may well be something or other that she hasn't thought to mention to me. You know how it is. Perhaps I could send a message round later to you?'

'I have a better notion, my dear Olivia,' said Mrs Allerton. 'Why do you not come and dine with us this evening — all of you, I mean? That is, of course, if Lydia should have recovered from her headache, for I know you won't like to leave her at home on her own if she feels unwell.'

'Oh, as to that,' replied Mrs Manbury, a fraction out of countenance, 'I think it was fatigue more than anything, and a good rest this morning will have put her right. Yes, I'm sure we shall all be delighted to come — thank you, my dear.'

'Can we count on you, Vivyan?' demanded his mother. 'Or have you some other engagement?'

'Oh, no, I shall be here,' he replied with alacrity, conveniently forgetting a half promise to meet some of his cronies at White's.

Mrs Allerton turned to Devenish. 'If you should chance to be free also, Sir James, we should be very happy — nothing formal, you understand, just a family party.'

Alethea, watching keenly, fancied that she could almost detect Beau Devenish repress a shudder at these words.

'You are too good, ma'am,' he answered smoothly, 'and nothing would give me greater pleasure. But unfortunately I am engaged for this evening.'

Mrs Allerton expressed her regret and hoped that perhaps it might be possible on another occasion.

He made a suitable reply before turning to Mrs Manbury and offering to take up Lydia and Alethea in his coach on the following day's expedition.

'That is, of course,' he concluded, 'if Miss Manbury does decide to go. Otherwise, I imagine Miss Newnham will be offered a place in your coach with your sisters, Allerton.'

This was agreed, and Alethea was left to draw the conclusion that it would not be proper for her to travel alone in a coach with Devenish. Evidently driving in the Park in an open carriage with a gentleman was quite another matter. She was learning fast about London ways, she reflected as her Aunt rose to leave.

After a brief interview with his father, Vivyan Allerton and his companion also left the house.

'A fine outing you persuaded me to!' he protested, as they strolled along. 'What the devil got into you? Historic buildings, good God!'

'A little culture, my dear fellow, will not come amiss with you, for once. It will make a change from gaming or watching mills and cockfights — not to speak of wenching.'

'A fine one you are to talk? I overheard Miss Newnham quizzing you about Vauxhall — I'll lay any odds you were there with one of your ladybirds, and she noticed your company. If so, doubtless Lydia did, too. That should sober you!'

'I'm not aware,' drawled Devenish, 'that I've given Miss Manbury any right to question what company I choose to keep.'

'Oh, Lud, no — I expect she knows as well as everyone else that she's just one of your flirts.'

Something in his tone caught Devenish's attention. 'Do you have a fancy there yourself, Vivyan?' he asked, quietly.

Allerton shrugged. 'Lud, what's the use? She's out for bigger game than me, I know that well enough.'

'I think you may be right, but I can safely promise you it won't be myself.' He hesitated, then said, diffidently for him, 'She's not worth it, you know, Viv. A spoilt brat, if ever there was one.'

'Yes, I do know, in a way. But —' he broke off, flushed slightly, then said with an attempt at cynicism — 'Oh, Lud, there's no logic in love! I'm not the only one to be at her feet, so at least I'm in the fashion.' He paused, evidently reluctant to say any more on that subject. 'What do you think of Miss Newnham?' he asked, after a moment. 'Quite an attractive girl, though not in her cousin's class, of course.'

'No,' replied Devenish, without appearing to consider the matter. 'She's decidedly in a class of her own.'

'You don't like her, I collect?'

'I should say rather that she dislikes me.'

Allerton started. 'You don't say so? Well, I must admit that does set her apart — never yet came across a female, old or young, who didn't fawn on you! No use to deny it, old fellow —' as Devenish made a gesture of distaste — 'You know it's true enough. Wouldn't surprise me if you don't see it as a challenge, if she really has taken you in dislike.'

'Possibly,' replied Devenish, drily. 'Yes, possibly I do.'

'So that's why!' said Allerton, with a chuckle. 'Historic buildings, indeed! You're a sly devil, ain't you?'

Chapter VII

When Mrs Manbury and Alethea returned home they found Lydia still inclined to be out of temper. She complained about the length of time they had been absent, and matters were not improved when she learnt that Beau Devenish had been at the Allertons' house.

'A fine thing that you should have been so well entertained while here was I sitting moped to death at home!' she exclaimed, petulantly.

'Whose fault is that, pray?' demanded her mother. 'I asked you to come with me, but you chose to stay at home.'

'Yes, but I didn't think anyone of interest would be there, and I wasn't in the mood for Felicia and Clarinda.'

'Well, it's a pity, my dear, but you've only yourself to blame. However, we've made some schemes for your entertainment — that is, if you care to join in. For one thing, we're all to dine at the Allertons' this evening —'

'Will Devenish be there?'

'No, for he has a previous engagement. But Vivyan will.'

Lydia shrugged. 'Oh, very well. But I don't call that a vastly entertaining scheme — was there anything else?'

With less assurance, Mrs Manbury went on to outline the plan for the following day. Lydia listened with incredulity bordering on indignation, and in the end demanded what in the world had made the Allertons hit on such a very odd scheme.

'I'm not perfectly certain how it started,' replied her mother, 'as I wasn't particularly attending at the time. Perhaps your cousin will know more about it.'

'I happened to mention that I would like to view some of London's famous buildings,' explained Alethea, in an apologetic tone. 'I had no notion that anyone would take me up.'

'I can't imagine who would!' said Lydia scornfully. 'Not either of the girls, I suppose — nor Vivyan, if I know him!'

'As a matter of fact, it was Clarinda,' said Alethea, 'and I thought it vastly good natured of her, for I don't believe she herself was really at all interested. She only suggested going because she thought to give me pleasure.'

'She is a prodigiously good hearted girl,' agreed Mrs Manbury. 'It's a pity that she's so plump.'

'But surely that doesn't detract from her good nature, Aunt?'

Mrs Manbury looked puzzled. 'What can you mean, child?'

'Oh, nothing,' replied Alethea, hastily, regretting her mistimed liveliness. 'Just nonsense — I beg your pardon.'

'So Clarinda said she'd go with you, and then the others decided to go, too — is that it?' asked Lydia. 'I must say, I'm puzzled that Devenish should have agreed to make one of the party.'

'It did seem to me,' remarked Mrs Manbury, 'that he was a prime mover in the scheme. I heard him point out to Vivyan that as Alethea so much wished to go, it would be ungallant to deny her the pleasure. Yes, and now I come to think of it, it was he who said why did they not make up a party. Wasn't it so, Alethea?'

Alethea assented and Lydia looked more mystified than before.

'I dare say, you know,' went on Mrs Manbury, 'that he was counting on your going with the rest, Lydia. You may be sure that was it.'

'Sir James Devenish has no right,' put in Lydia, loftily, 'to count on my doing anything or going anywhere to oblige him. I am completely indifferent to him, and the sooner he realises that, the better.'

'To be sure, love, but he's not indifferent to you, as anyone may see.'

'His attentions mean nothing as you very well know, Mama, since you are always reminding me of it. Only consider the company we saw him in at Vauxhall! I wonder he can expect any genteel female will so much as speak to him after that!'

'Nonsense, Lydia. You are too severe. You know very well how it is with gentlemen — a well bred girl doesn't notice such things, so I advise you to put it right out of your mind. And on no account must you make any reference to it, so pray keep a guard on your tongue when next you meet him.'

Alethea could only feel thankful that her own oblique remarks to Beau Devenish on this subject had not been overheard by her aunt. No doubt she, too, would have been given a scold. Lydia merely shrugged, knowing very well that her mother was right. She had no intention of making any direct reference to the incident at Vauxhall, but she thought there might be other ways of showing her disapproval to Devenish. One of these, she decided with a flash of inspiration, could be employed tomorrow, did she choose to accompany the others on their expedition. She was very well aware that Vivyan Allerton had long been a serious admirer of hers; it was time she offered him a little encouragement. A judicious flirtation with Vivyan should soon put Devenish firmly in his place.

This reflection did a great deal to restore her good humour; which was just as well, because it was not long before a visitor was announced.

'Mr Paul Tracy,' repeated Mrs Manbury, frowning over the card. 'Now, who —?'

'Oh,' said Alethea, quickly. 'It is a gentleman Miss More and I met at Mrs Montagu's. He very kindly offered to lend me a book we were discussing and I expect that's why he has called.'

Mrs Manbury looked at her niece keenly, but could see no sign of self-consciousness. She instructed the footman to show the gentleman up, and presently Mr Tracy entered the room, carrying a slim volume in his hand.

Alethea rose to greet him and present him to her aunt and cousin. He acknowledged the introductions with a grave bow to each lady, then laying the book on a small table at Alethea's side, obeyed Mrs Manbury's injunction to be seated.

Some small talk followed, in which Lydia played a lively part, bestowing her dimpling smiles freely on the visitor in what was to her a routine reaction to any male. In spite of this, Mrs Manbury noticed with surprise that his eyes went more frequently to Alethea's face than to her cousin's. She told herself that she must inquire into this gentleman's background. Whatever notions the girl herself might hold on the subject, Mrs Manbury at least had no doubt of the real reason why Alethea had been sent to stay with her in London. Her sister Cassandra was seeking an eligible husband for this daughter of hers, and Mrs Manbury was quite willing to play her part in the affair. Up to now, though, she had been a little daunted by the fact that Alethea was an unusual type of girl. She was too bookish by half, and seemed to have no notion of how to play off those little feminine wiles which most girls could readily employ to enslave men. Then, too, she could not compare to Lydia in looks. There was a certain cool attractiveness about her, Mrs Manbury decided, watching her niece as she chatted easily to the visitor. Although brown hair must be thought ordinary enough, Alethea's had interesting reddish glints which sprang to life in sun or candlelight. Her face was piquant at times, and her clear grey eyes were undeniably expressive. In short, if Lydia had only been missing, Alethea might almost have passed for a beauty.

But it seemed that here was one man, at any rate, who liked the girl's oddities, and even preferred to gaze at her rather than at her more attractive cousin. Decidedly, he ought to be encouraged, thought Mrs Manbury, should he prove eligible as far as birth and fortune were concerned. In any other way, she reflected, he could scarcely be considered a great catch. His dress, though of good quality, had none of the marks of fashion which distinguished Devenish and his set. His hesitant manner of speech, with his 'Um' and 'Ah', the frequent pauses and apologetic little laughs, she found irritating in the extreme. Still, he would do well enough for Alethea, who with her odd ways and bookishness could scarcely hope to win a husband of fashion and poise. As long as he was a man of substance and breeding; Mrs Manbury felt she owed it to her family to satisfy herself on this point.

Deep in conversation, the two people whose future she was settling remained mercifully unconscious of the trend of her thoughts. The talk had turned to the theatre, and Mr Tracey was again extolling the acting of Mrs Siddons.

'I heard so much said in her praise at Mrs Montagu's soiree!' exclaimed Alethea. 'I declare I'm dying to see her act for myself.'

'Well, and why not?' rejoined Lydia. 'It's true she's all the rage. Mama, why don't we go to the play — when we have nothing better to do, that is?'

Mrs Manbury said that this could be arranged, and turning graciously to Mr Tracy, asked him if he would care to make one of the party. He stammered out an awkward but obviously eager acceptance, and presently rose to take his leave.

'What an odd creature!' remarked Lydia with a giggle, when he had gone and her mother had left the room.

'I do not find him odd,' retorted Alethea. 'And I'm told that he is a writer of some merit.'

'Oh, but my dear cousin, all that stammering and those absurd little titters of his!' And she pranced up and down the room, giving a very fair imitation of Paul Tracy's conversational manner.

Alethea could not help smiling. 'Well, I'll admit that his mannerisms take a little getting used to. But the matter of his conversation is so full of interest, that one soon forgets the manner.'

'Well, I was fit to burst my sides, I assure you!'

'Let me congratulate you, then, for concealing your mirth so well,' replied Alethea drily.

'Oh, pooh! One learns that kind of thing in the nursery. But never tell me that you admire him, Alethea! And after meeting such beaux as Devenish and Calver, or even Vivyan Allerton!'

'I am not yet sufficiently acquainted with any of the gentlemen you mention to say whether or not they are admirable,' said Alethea, coldly. 'Although as far as Sir James Devenish is concerned —'

'Yes? What have you to say of Beau Devenish?'

'Simply that nothing you have told me of him leads me to expect it. And from what I've seen myself, he seems to be nothing but a — a fashion plate!' finished Alethea defiantly.

Lydia looked annoyed for a moment, then laughed. 'Well, it's plain to see we differ in our tastes as far as gentlemen are concerned. Maybe it's just as well,' she added, reflectively. 'Although to tell the truth, cousin, I am not best pleased with

Devenish myself at present. I shall teach him a lesson, though, you'll see. But why on earth should Mama have asked that odd little Tracy man to join us at the theatre, I wonder? Let's hope she means to include someone more lively in the party, as well.'

Alethea made no reply to this, but an unwelcome suspicion crossed her mind. She dismissed it firmly, settling down to write a letter home.

The evening at the Allertons' was pleasant, with that relaxed, informal atmosphere only possible when people are intimately acquainted. The only guest who was not a member of either family was Lord Calver, whom Vivyan had invited, so he asserted, to keep him in countenance among so many young ladies. Calver had accepted the invitation with alacrity; but this was no surprise to Vivyan, as for some weeks now he had noticed that Calver was betraying a certain interest in Felicia.

After dinner was over, the older members of the party settled down to cards, leaving the young people to entertain themselves as they chose. They chatted together for a while, and then Calver suggested some music.

He urged Felicia to play for them, but she had a better notion of her duty as a hostess than to sit down first to the pianoforte. Lydia was soon persuaded to sing a duet with Vivyan; they rendered this in such a melting style, that Alethea laughingly confessed herself quite unable to follow them. Accordingly, Felicia then sat down to play a piece of Scarlatti's. She was an accomplished pianist, and even the card players raised their heads once or twice while she was performing. When she had finished, the applause was sincere, and everyone begged for an encore; but she shook her head, smiling and saying to Alethea, 'Now it's your turn, Miss Newnham.'

'How in the world can you suppose it's any easier for me to follow *that*?' asked Alethea, in laughing dismay. 'I'll tell you what — I'll play some airs for the rest of you to sing.'

This suggestion was greeted with enthusiasm, and soon the drawing room resounded to their voices. The card party did not seem quite so appreciative of this part of the performance, and were not sorry when lack of breath caused the singers to bring it to an end. Mrs Allerton rang for the tea tray to be brought in, and not long afterwards the party broke up; Vivyan and Calver going off to one of the clubs to finish the evening, which as far as they were concerned was still young.

'Very pleasant — very pleasant indeed,' pronounced Mrs Manbury, as their carriage bore them homewards. 'There is nothing so restful as a quiet dinner with old friends.'

Everyone agreed with this sentiment.

'Did you notice, Mama, how Felicia was making up to Calver?' asked Lydia, after an interval.

'I would say rather that it was the other way about. She behaved with perfect propriety, as far as I could see.'

'Oh, well,' said Lydia, with a shrug, 'I'm not saying she didn't, precisely. I dare say she fancies he is in love with her.'

'And why should he not be?' asked her father, indulgently. 'She's a charming enough girl, and it's time Calver was looking out for a wife. I know what it is, puss,' he added, giving Lydia a playful dig, 'you want all the young men for yourself! But there are more than enough of 'em trailing after you as it is, so you've no cause to fret if one gets away. In my view, you'd best settle on one of 'em soon, and put the other poor devils out of their misery!'

Lydia dimpled prettily at him, pleased with this speech, then settled back against the seat to consider tomorrow's expedition.

She had quite made up her mind to offer Devenish the cold shoulder, and this evening had shown her how easy it would be to start up a counter flirtation with Vivyan. Calver was to join the party, but that was all to the good, for he could evidently be counted on to monopolise most of Felicia's attention. That would leave Devenish with Clarinda, who bored him, and Alethea, who disliked him and never quite managed to hide the fact. And serve him right, thought Lydia, with relish. He richly deserved a set-down.

Chapter VIII

Seated opposite the two young ladies in his fashionable town coach on the following morning, Beau Devenish reflected that there must be many less pleasant ways of passing one's time. Certainly they presented a picture to charm the most fastidious eye, Lydia dainty and fresh in a white muslin gown embroidered with tiny pink flowers, and Alethea wearing green, which brought out the auburn tints in her hair.

'You may perhaps care to glance at this,' he said, languidly, handing Lydia a small book and making sure that his fingers touched hers as she accepted it.

'What is it?' she asked. 'Oh, a guide book — how can you suppose, Sir James, that I should wish to study anything so prosy? You may have it, Alethea, if you wish.'

Ignoring the implication of this, Alethea took the book and turned to the section in it dealing with St Paul's Cathedral. She began to read, knowing that in leaving the other two to talk together she was behaving just as Lydia would wish.

After a while, she glanced up to study them for a moment, as it did seem that Lydia was not quite so ebullient as usual. Devenish's manner was, as always, elegantly languid; but his eyes were admiring her cousin in a way that sent a quick tingle down Alethea's spine. Could this be flirting? It was obvious that Lydia fascinated him, but possibly he was equally fascinated by other pretty girls, and eyed them all in the same way. She acknowledged to herself that she knew nothing of the matter, and, after all, it did not concern her; so she resumed her reading until she had come to the end of the section on St Paul's. She looked up then to see Devenish's eyes on her, though certainly not with the same expression in them that Lydia had produced.

'Do you feel qualified now to act as our guide, Miss Newnham?' he asked.

'On the strength of ten minutes' reading, sir? I only hope I'm not so arrogant,' she laughed.

'It was not my intention to suggest you were, ma'am. But you've been reading with intense concentration — no easy matter in a moving vehicle, I may add — so you must be tolerably well-informed on the subject.'

'Oh, my cousin's a prodigious reader,' put in Lydia. 'But there's no need, Alethea, to concern yourself with such stuff — anything you wish to know, I dare say one of the guides will inform you. Not,' she added, 'that we would wish to go round with one of those creatures in tow, prosing on for ever!'

'Will you be content, then, with what information Allerton, Calver and I may be able to supply?' he asked her, with a twinkle in his eye.

'Perfectly, for I've no wish to turn the visit into a schoolroom exercise. I can't speak for Alethea, of course. She may have different notions.'

'Well, here we are,' remarked Devenish, evading a reply to this as the coach drew up before the steps of the Cathedral. 'And there are the others, just alighting — what could be better?'

He helped the girls down from the coach, and Alethea stood for a moment to admire the majestic building with its great cupola surmounted by a cross. Vivyan Allerton had come over to Lydia's side at once, and was offering his arm to assist her in mounting the steps. She accepted with a tantalising backward glance at Devenish which he seemed not to notice, and together she and Vivyan began the ascent. Calver had already started up the steps with the Allerton girls, leaving Alethea standing with Devenish.

'May I assist you, ma'am?' he asked with a slight bow.

She hesitated, then placed her hand lightly on his arm, feeling as she did so that she was touching fire. This absurd fancy so annoyed her that, by the time they reached the top of the steps, she was frowning heavily. He glanced down at her, thinking wryly that for all his reputed success with women, he had failed singly here. It was evident that Alethea Newnham had taken him in strong dislike. Well, as Allerton had said, it was more of a challenge.

They passed through the doors into the Cathedral, and were approached by a guide who offered his services. Lydia pouted and tugged at Allerton's arm, trying to persuade him to turn the man away.

'We shall be here for ever if once we let him show us round,' she whispered. 'Do, pray, get rid of him!'

The whisper was sufficiently loud for it to reach the guide's ears, and he undertook to be brief, as it seemed that the ladies and gentlemen were pressed for time. With this undertaking, he was allowed to lead them round; but Lydia was not pleased, and showed it by detaching herself from the rest of the group and walking a little way ahead with Vivyan, who had eyes for nothing and no one but her.

'It is a truly magnificent nave,' remarked Alethea, gazing towards the high altar. 'Only look at those arches!'

'Yes, indeed,' Devenish replied. 'It is melancholy to reflect that at one time it was used as a passageway, with horses being led through, colliers carrying sacks of coal, and so on.'

They all exclaimed in horror.

'Pray, how do you know that?' demanded Lydia, who happened at that moment to be close enough to hear what he was saying.

'Oh, I have been here before, you know,' he said, in his usual languid manner. 'On that occasion, I recall being shown round by a guide who was evidently determined that I shouldn't leave the building without carrying in my memory every smallest detail concerning it.'

Their present guide, somewhat on his mettle, here interrupted to say that the gentleman was quite right, such had been the practice in the old building; but although it was revived in the new one, Bishop Gibson had put a stop to it some sixty years ago. He then led them slowly down the nave coming to a halt beneath the great dome. Here they all gazed upwards while he talked about the paintings surrounding the inner dome, which represented scenes in the life of St Paul. After a moment, Lydia complained that to look up in that way made her neck ache excruciatingly; so she walked away, accepting Vivyan's arm.

Alethea expressed a wish to go up into the Whispering Gallery, but the other young ladies disliked the thought of mounting so many stairs, so she did not persist. They passed into the choir, and here the guide called on them to admire the handsome carvings of Grinling Gibbons and the magnificent ironwork of Jean Tijou in the sanctuary gates. When they had paused before the effigy of Dr John Donne and finally stood gazing at the high altar, Lydia began to exhibit further signs of impatience.

'Surely we have been here long enough now! I declare we must have seen everything there is to see! If we are to go anywhere else, we'd best be on our way — although, for my part, I'm ready to own that I've done more than enough sightseeing for one day.'

'If we might just go into the crypt,' pleaded Alethea. 'Christopher Wren is buried there, and I feel that his memory merits some attention.'

Lydia shuddered. 'The crypt! It sounds vastly disagreeable, and is sure to be dirty.'

Felicia and Clarinda were inclined to agree with her; but Clarinda nobly volunteered to accompany Alethea while the others remained seated in the nave to await them.

'No, too shabby,' murmured Calver. 'I'll come, too, Miss Newnham.'

As they all three turned to follow the guide, they were joined by Devenish, somewhat to Alethea's surprise. In the south aisle of the crypt they found the simple grave of the architect, and stood there for a moment in silence.

'His son, who was also Christopher,' the guide informed them, 'composed this epitaph *Si monumentum requiris circumspice* — and that, ladies, means —'

'"If you seek his monument, look about you" — yes, how very true,' said Alethea, spontaneously. 'This building will be an everlasting memorial to a great architect.'

As they were making their way back to join the others, Devenish remarked, 'You must have attended a somewhat unusual Ladies' Seminary, Miss Newnham.'

'Why do you think so?' she asked, surprised.

'Because you appear to have some Latin. Not a usual accomplishment for a young lady, I believe.'

'Oh, but I didn't learn that at school. Papa taught me himself — I am the only girl in a family of boys, you see, and he educated me in just the same way as the rest before I went to the Misses More's Seminary, later on.'

She stopped suddenly, thinking that he would be bored. From what she had seen of him with others, she had concluded that he had little interest in details of anyone's personal affairs.

'So you have been brought up in an all-male household?' he asked, without betraying any noticeable signs of boredom. 'Ah, that may account for much.'

'What do you mean, sir? It's a somewhat equivocal remark,' she replied, smiling up at him.

He gave an answering smile that for once seemed free of mockery. 'I suppose it is, and I ought to beg your pardon for thinking aloud. Let me assure you, though, that my thoughts were wholly complimentary towards you. And since I am quite sure that you won't now insist on learning what I did mean, I shall take leave to inform you without being asked. I meant that such an upbringing would account for that total lack of female affectation which is charming in you, ma'am. Not to say refreshing,' he added.

She turned her head away, hardly knowing how to answer this, and thankful that they joined the rest of the party at that moment, thus relieving her of the necessity. All the same, she felt a little less hostile towards him, in spite of herself. This more favourable impression lasted during a visit to Westminster Abbey which was too short for Alethea, although quite long enough for most of the party.

Lydia relieved her boredom by continuing her promising flirtation with Vivyan Allerton. From time to time, she would glance covertly at Devenish to see how he was taking it, but he gave no sign of noticing. He chatted now and then to all the others, but he gave most of his attention to Alethea; offering information on what they saw whenever she asked for it, and surprising her by the extent of his knowledge on matters to which she would have supposed him completely indifferent. She could scarcely believe that this was the same man who thought of nothing but dress and the elegant — or perhaps not so elegant, she amended, remembering Vauxhall — pursuits of the man about Town.

On leaving the Abbey, both Lydia and Felicia insisted that they were much too fatigued to endure any more sight-seeing that day, so it was decided to postpone a visit to the Tower which had been on their list. The Allertons pressed their friends to return home with them to partake of some refreshment; and, after some polite disclaimers, the invitation was accepted. Once they were sitting down to an appetising meal of cold meat, fruits and small cakes, fatigue seemed forgotten, and they were quite a merry party. Lydia still continued to flirt with Allerton, and it was obvious to everyone present that he was rapidly becoming completely infatuated by her. Devenish observed them cynically from time to time, but, greatly to Lydia's secret disappointment, gave not the slightest hint of pique at having lost her favour.

When the party finally broke up, he conveyed the two cousins home in his coach.

'I trust, Miss Newnham,' he said, smiling lazily at her, 'that you feel able to say now that you've seen something of London.'

'Indeed I do, sir, and I'm most grateful to you and to the Allertons for taking the trouble to show me round,' she replied warmly.

He bowed. 'A pleasure, I assure you.'

'Well,' remarked Lydia, stifling a yawn, 'it wasn't near such a dull day as I had feared, I must say. But then, anything can be amusing in the right company, would you not agree?' she added, with a touch of malice.

'Undoubtedly.' There was a cynical look in his eye.

'I had forgot how entertaining Vivyan can be,' she went on. 'As our families are such close friends, we were often together as children, but we haven't seen much of each other more recently.'

'You must certainly renew your acquaintance,' he answered, smoothly. 'He is the best of fellows.'

She gave a petulant little shrug and turned to Alethea. 'I knew it would be dusty in those places! See, the hem of my gown is quite soiled — how tiresome!'

'Is it? But then, a white gown soon soils. I didn't notice any dust.'

'If we chance to visit the Tower,' remarked Devenish, 'we must send first to request that the building should be thoroughly swept and dusted.'

Lydia's eyes flashed. 'If you think to make game of me, Sir James —'

'I, make game of you?' He raised his hands in horror. 'My dear young lady, I wouldn't have the temerity to attempt anything so abominable.'

'Ay, so you say, but I don't believe it! Do you, Alethea?'

Alethea hesitated. Undoubtedly Devenish was poking fun at her cousin; but this was a lovers' quarrel in which she had too much good sense to become involved. At least, they were not precisely lovers, she corrected herself; there was more of vanity than love in their association.

'How can I say?' she temporised. 'Sir James Devenish and I have only just met. But I know you are fatigued, Lydia, and I'm sorry for it, as it's on my account.'

'Pray don't regard it,' replied Lydia, snappishly. 'We shall soon be home, thank goodness.'

After this ungracious remark, there was silence in the coach for several minutes. Devenish broke it by picking up the guide book from the seat beside him and handing it to Alethea. With this young lady, he was careful to see that their fingers did not make contact.

'Perhaps you may care to keep this, Miss Newnham.'

She took the book with a quick smile. 'How very kind of you, sir! It will be most useful. It was stupid of me not to have provided myself with one before coming to London, but it was something I forgot.'

'I dare say Papa may have one in the library,' put in Lydia. 'I do not know I'm sure — such things don't interest me.' She put up her gloved hand to stifle a second yawn.

Another silence fell over them, and Alethea took the opportunity to glance through the book. She noticed what she had missed before, a name inscribed on the fly leaf 'James R. Devenish'. She glanced across at Devenish in some dismay.

'But this is your own copy!' she exclaimed. 'I cannot take it.'

He dismissed her objection with a wave of his hand.

'Pray do, ma'am — Assure you I shall be much honoured.'

Lydia looked daggers, and Alethea found herself blushing. She was conscious of being used much as Vivyan Allerton had been and she disliked it extremely.

Chapter IX

The next morning was not far advanced when the two Allerton girls came to call in Curzon Street accompanied by their brother Vivyan. Caroline Fothergill, who had just looked in upon her mother on her way to do some shopping, raised her eyebrows when the callers were announced.

'Well, 'pon 'rep, haven't you just been telling me that you were with the Allertons most of yesterday? And since when has Vivyan Allerton started squiring his sisters about Town? Have we you to thank for this, Alethea? You must have made a prodigious impression upon him, my dear cousin — and in St Paul's Cathedral, of all places!'

Lydia looked displeased. Alethea smiled and shook her head, but had no time to say anything in reply before the visitors entered the room. It was not long before Caroline saw her mistake and realised that it was her sister whom Allerton had come to see. Today he was taking no pains to disguise the admiration which he had long felt for Lydia, but which he had previously tried to keep hidden.

Lydia herself, outwardly all smiles and charm, felt some inner qualms. Perhaps she had been rather too encouraging to Vivyan yesterday, in her determination to give Devenish a set-down. It would be a pity if he had gathered a false impression of her interest in him. She had no wish to bring on a declaration in that quarter; the inevitable refusal might make relations between the two families a trifle awkward. Why could not the stupid fellow understand that she had only been indulging in one of her light-hearted flirtations? How difficult men were, to be sure, always ready to believe that a girl was only waiting to throw herself at their heads! It was so much simpler with someone like Devenish, who understood the game.

Allerton was pressing her now to come driving with him in the Park that afternoon, and for once she was not at all sure how to answer. She glanced at her mother for assistance, but Mrs Manbury saw no harm in the company of a young man who had always been regarded almost in the light of a relative. Fortunately, Lydia was saved from an immediate reply by the arrival of yet another visitor. This time it was Mr Paul Tracy.

'Um — er — I beg your pardon, Mrs Manbury,' he stammered, hesitating as he saw other visitors present. 'I would not — um — have intruded upon you had I realised — er — that is to say — I believed that possibly at this hour, I might — um, er — perhaps find you —'

'Not at all, sir,' said Mrs Manbury, deciding that she could not possibly wait for the conclusion of this speech. 'We are almost a family party here, for these are some very intimate friends whom we have known for ever. Permit me to make them known to you.'

Paul Tracy acknowledged the introductions in his awkward, apologetic way, still looking ill at ease. Mrs Manbury steered him to a seat next to Alethea, wisely leaving it to her niece to soothe his ruffled sensibilities. This Alethea managed by talking at first on that stock British subject, the weather. Gradually he relaxed sufficiently to ask her about the book he had lent her.

'Oh, I've finished it,' she replied, 'but I've laid it by for a few days so that I can give it a second reading. One misses so much the first time, don't you agree?'

He did, and went on to compare *The Village* with Goldsmith's poem on a similar subject and with Gray's *Elegy in a Country Churchyard.*

'Simplicity — er — and truth are Crabbe's driving forces,' stated Mr Tracy, with energy. 'He employs — um — no tricks to engage our senses as these others do — um — er — he idealises nothing.'

'So much I have noticed,' agreed Alethea, 'But I must confess that at times I found myself wishing that he didn't view everything in quite such a dismal way. I fear you'll never disenchant me with Gray, Mr Tracy. I still admire the *Elegy* in spite of having read Crabbe's work — though possibly such an admission will make you think me sadly lacking in taste.'

'By — by no means, ma'am,' stuttered Mr Tracy with emphasis. 'I do not mean to say — um — that there are not some memorable lines in the *Elegy*, or that Gray is unworthy — er — of serious consideration as a poet. No, far be it from me — um — As for yourself, Miss Newnham,' here he seemed to experience some difficulty in continuing at all — 'um — er — no one could doubt — er — that is to say — your taste must seem superior —'

Lydia, who was once again being pressed by Vivyan to go out with him that afternoon, here broke in upon their conversation. 'What in the world can you and Mr Tracy be discussing so very earnestly, Alethea?' she demanded, laughing.

'Only a book which Mr Tracy was good enough to lend me.'

'Oh, a book! People are for ever lending you books, it seems — or giving them to you,' said Lydia, with a hint of spitefulness.

'Why, who has given you a book, Alethea?' asked her Aunt.

'Well, it was just that Sir James Devenish said I might keep the guide book we were making use of yesterday, that is all,' replied Alethea, carelessly.

'You forgot to say, though, that it was his own copy,' Lydia reminded her.

'Devenish?' repeated Vivyan, incredulously. 'Devenish possessed a guide book to London? Well, if that don't beat all!'

'I'm sure I don't see why he should not,' said Mrs Manbury. 'Such things have their uses, particularly if one should be entertaining friends from the country or from foreign shores.'

'Very true, ma'am — but Devenish! I must say I don't see him in the guise of mentor and guide!'

'Ah, well, possibly you don't know him as well as you think, Vivyan,' replied Mrs Manbury. 'For my part, I've long since ceased to be surprised at anything people may say or do. One can never tell, even with one's own family, much less with one's acquaintance.'

Caroline laughed. 'You may have some justification for that point of view, Mama, for I'm sure I never know myself for five minutes together how I intend to act!' She glanced at the ormolu clock on the mantelshelf. 'Heavens, I must fly! I've shopping to do and an appointment for this afternoon that cannot be broken. Lydia, don't forget that we've fixed on Monday for our visit to the play. Fothergill has bespoken a box, and we shall expect you round to dine with us first.'

'I did ask you, Mr Tracy, if you would care to join us when we decided to visit the theatre,' said Mrs Manbury, turning towards him. 'I do trust that you may chance to be free on Monday evening? I am sorry that it should be such short notice.'

He managed to stammer out an acceptance, and Caroline hospitably included him in the invitation to dinner.

'I haven't yet seen the Incomparable Sarah myself,' put in Vivyan, reflectively. 'Everyone tells me I should —'

'Oh, yes, Viv, there's no doubt of it at all!' enthused Felicia. 'Clarry was so overcome when we last went to see *The Fatal Marriage* that she cried all the way home! And I honestly don't think there was a dry eye in the whole audience at the end of the play — Mrs Siddons was magnificent — so moving, and such dignity in her afflictions!'

'Well, I don't promise to emulate Clarry,' said her brother, laughing. 'But all the same, the Siddons is a great actress, by all accounts, and the season will soon be over. I don't suppose —' he paused, suggestively.

'Why, of course,' Caroline took him up at once. 'We shall have room, and George would like you to join us. We are taking the girls, you know, as Mama doesn't wish to go herself. Will you dine with us first, along with the others? Do — it will make a pleasant-sized party, and even numbers, too.'

Caroline's departure was the signal for the others to leave, although Vivyan Allerton did not do so until he had secured Lydia's promise to drive with him that afternoon. At first she tried to excuse herself on the grounds that she did not like to leave Alethea at home, but Alethea soon disposed of this by saying that she would be glad of an opportunity to write some letters.

'You might have supported me,' Lydia grumbled, when the visitors had gone. 'You must know that I don't choose to be private with Vivyan.'

'No, how should I?' demanded Alethea. 'Only yesterday, you seemed set on that very thing!'

'You know perfectly well why that was. I told you I meant to give Devenish a set-down.'

'Forgive me, Lydia, but I refuse to be made a party to your intrigues.'

'Oh, you're such a prude!' snapped Lydia, the lovely face drawn into a disfiguring scowl. 'I only hope you make a match of it with that stupid oaf of a poet, for you'll be very well suited, the pair of you!'

'I'm not looking to make a match of it with anyone,' retorted Alethea.

'Then you're stupid, as well, for what else can one do but marry? Except become an old maid,' she added, with a scornful laugh, 'and that wouldn't suit me, though I can quite see that it might be the very thing for you.'

'Well, perhaps it might. I really don't know. But what I do know is that I find the concentration of all one's thoughts, aspirations and energies on the subject of matrimony so tedious that it cannot be borne! For pity's sake,' went on Alethea, warmly, 'are there not other subjects capable of inspiring interest, other channels for one's thoughts? And after so much time and scheming being devoted to achieving a marriage what could it ever be but a miserable anti-climax? What is there left? Your own sister —' She broke off, then continued apologetically — 'but perhaps I've no right to speak of that. Although we are cousins, we do not yet know each other very well.'

'Oh, Caroline,' said Lydia, with a shrug. 'Yes, you may discuss her with me, if you wish. It doesn't offend me in the slightest.'

'Well, you can't claim that she is very happy; and yet, by my Aunt's account, a deal of scheming went into her marriage.'

'I think she's well enough suited,' replied Lydia, indifferently. 'Fothergill is dull, of course, but then most husbands are. She has a comfortable and elegant establishment, and wants for nothing.'

'Except for the companionship of a partner whom she can both love and respect,' said Alethea, with emphasis.

'Oh, fie! You ask too much. Most marriages are matters of convenience — one is unusually fortunate if love enters into the bargain.'

'If that is so, then I am less than ever inclined towards "making a match of it", as you say — at least, on your terms.'

Lydia stared, then burst out laughing. 'Dear sakes, never say that you're of a romantic turn of mind! You with your bookishness and forthright views — no, that's too much! My poor cousin, for all you're a deal cleverer than I am, it seems you've much to learn about the ways of the world.'

'Doubtless,' said Alethea, and went out of the room.

Later, when Vivyan Allerton had taken Lydia out for a drive and Mrs Manbury was resting in her room, Alethea sat down to write a letter home. She gave a lively account of all that had been happening during the past few days, and then went on in a more serious vein.

I must say, Mama, that so far my cousin and I do not get on too well. Perhaps it is my fault. She is the complete town lady, while I am something of a country mouse. But our standards are so different, and I think must remain so, however much "town polish" I may manage to acquire, Harry would have it that you also sent me to London to catch a husband (I am using his phrase, so do not chide me!) and my cousin and Aunt seem to be of the same opinion.

I know it is all nonsense and you never could have had any such motive; but at times I cannot help feeling vexed with Lydia and my Aunt for persisting in the notion. A word from you might save me some embarrassment in this respect.

However, do not think, dearest Mama, that I am not enjoying myself. I live in a constant whirl of pleasure and meet such a great variety of people that every day my experience is extended and my mind stimulated. Papa would remind me, I know, that this can never be an entirely comfortable process, although it does one good. I only hope I am not too much changed when next you see me! Give my fond love to Papa and the boys, and do let me know when Sukey has her kittens.

Ever your affectionate daughter,
Alethea.

Chapter X

After all the objections that Lydia had raised to driving out with Allerton, Alethea was surprised to find her engaged for a similar expedition on the following day. Mrs Manbury ventured to comment on this seeming change of attitude, but Lydia replied with an easy — 'Oh, I was quite mistaken, Mama! I see now that I can manage Vivyan with the greatest ease in the world.'

'And I dare say she may,' remarked Alethea's Aunt, after Allerton had called and borne Lydia away. 'Most of the men are wild for her, you know, because I must admit — although she's my own, and perhaps I shouldn't — that she's an uncommonly attractive girl. But she has her head screwed on the right way, and always knows to a nicety how to avoid an unwanted declaration. Not that there could be the least objection to Vivyan, of course, in the ordinary way. He has an independent fortune besides what will come to him on his father's death; and as to birth, that is impeccable. But any female with Lydia's looks can aspire to a truly brilliant match; and, after all, a girl must do the best she can for herself, don't you agree?'

'Oh, certainly,' said Alethea, drily. 'The only point on which I fear we may differ, Aunt, is just what precisely *is* the best.'

Mrs Manbury stared. 'Really, you are a very singular girl, Alethea! You must know well enough what I mean. I don't mind telling you in confidence that we have great hopes of the Duke of Bedwyn, so you will readily see that Lydia's other suitors cannot be encouraged until we know just how matters stand in that quarter. At present he is away at his Lincolnshire estate, but he should be returning before long, and then we shall see.'

'Does Lydia favour this gentleman?'

'But naturally, my dear. Who would not favour a Duke?' replied Mrs Manbury, surprised.

'I was thinking of the man rather than the title. What manner of man is he?' persisted Alethea. 'Is he as personable as, say, Mr Allerton or Sir James Devenish?'

'Oh, well, no, for he is a good deal older than either. He has been twice married before, and has daughters by both marriages, but no son. Naturally, he wants an heir; and if he can take one of the Town's reigning belles as a third wife, I believe he, too, will think he has made a good bargain.'

A good bargain! So marriage was simply a matter of buying and selling, thought Alethea contemptuously. But even the short time she had spent in her Aunt's household had taught her the futility of voicing the thought. She glanced out of the window. It would be so much pleasanter out of doors in this sunny weather. At home, she would have been out in the garden, or else walking in one of the leafy lanes near the village. Here in London, however, a young lady could not wander through the streets unattended. She sighed as she picked up a book and settled down to read.

Mrs Manbury had just decided to go up to her room for a rest when a visitor was announced. She clicked her tongue in annoyance as she scanned the card presented by her footman, but nevertheless she told the man to admit the caller.

'So vexing — it's Devenish of all people, and Lydia out with Vivyan Allerton! Not that I don't think it a good thing for her association with Devenish to come to an end. Well, I shall soon get rid of him, you'll see.'

Beau Devenish, elegant as usual, was with them before Alethea could make any answer to this. It was soon made clear, however, that he had not come in search of Lydia. He was well aware that she was out driving with Allerton, as he had met them in the Park and stayed to chat with them for a while. In the course of their conversation, he said, he had learned that Miss Newnham was spending the afternoon quietly at home with her Aunt.

'And so, ma'am,' he concluded, turning his most persuasive smile upon Mrs Manbury, 'it occurred to me that possibly your niece might also prefer to be out of doors in this quite delightful weather. If so, I should be happy — with your approval — to take Miss Newnham for a short drive.'

Mrs Manbury gave him a shrewd, calculating look. 'Very handsome of you, Sir James. Alethea, what do you say? Would you care to go?'

Alethea hesitated. She had been taken by surprise, and was not quite sure how to answer. Although she was longing to be out of doors, she certainly had no wish for Devenish's company.

'It is very good of Sir James, ma'am, but I would not like to leave you on your own.'

'Nonsense, child, you need not regard that. You must know that I am always best pleased if I can take a rest at this hour of the day. At my time of life one cannot burn the candle at both ends and one's evenings are often so fatiguing, don't you agree, Sir James?'

'Prodigiously fatiguing, ma'am,' he drawled, 'and frequently a dead bore into the bargain.' He turned to Alethea, an ironical smile on his lips. 'So you see, Miss Newnham, you need consult nothing but your own inclination.'

Put like this, she could scarcely refuse him and soon he was handing her up into a smart phaeton with yellow wheels. A groom who had been left in charge of the horses was dismissed with a nod. Devenish took up the reins, and the equipage moved smoothly forward in the direction of the Park.

For a time, there was silence between them. The streets were busy, and most of Devenish's attention was on his driving. As for Alethea, she felt that she had been outmanoeuvred, and consequently was in no mood to initiate a conversation.

As they passed through the gate into the Park, he turned towards her and said 'A penny for your thoughts, ma'am.'

'They're not worth it,' she replied, with a shrug.

'No, I suppose not — to me at any rate.' He gave her a smile that was less ironical than usual, so that for a moment she fancied she caught a glimpse of quite another man from the elegant, languid Beau Devenish. It was gone again before she could make any mental adjustment. 'I think I can safely hazard a guess about them, however,' he concluded. The smile broadened, inviting her to respond.

She refused to be drawn. 'Indeed, sir?'

He laughed and flung up an arm as though to defend himself from a blow. 'Egad, are you so very displeased? I knew you were thinking me a tiresome fellow for forcing your hand just now, but I ventured to hope that once we were out driving, you might think better of it — and of me.'

'You are quite correct in supposing that I don't care to have my hand forced,' retorted Alethea, coldly.

'But, had I not forced the issue,' he protested, easing the horses to a quiet pace which made few claims on his attention, 'you would have refused me, wouldn't you?'

She made no answer.

'Come; you were given the name Alethea, and that means "Truth", does it not?'

She nodded. 'But I've learnt, sir, that truth is a commodity to be dealt in sparingly.'

'Well, I concede you that, in a general way, of course. In this instance, you may safely answer my question truthfully, however. I promise not to take offence.'

'Why should I put myself to so much trouble, when you seem to know the answer?' She relented sufficiently to give him a small, twisted smile.

'So you would have refused to come? May I ask why?'

'You may, but I don't undertake to reply.' She spoke repressively.

He surveyed her with an amused light in his eyes. 'I do believe, Miss Newnham — odd as it may seem — that you dislike me,' he stated, in his most elegant drawl.

'I hardly know you, Sir James.'

'But obviously you dislike what you do know. Pray tell me, ma'am, what I have done to incur your displeasure?'

'You talk a deal of nonsense, sir!' She flushed a little under his amused scrutiny. 'Pray let us discuss some other topic.'

'But of course! You don't like nonsense, I collect? You never indulge in any conversation of which the great Dr Johnson himself would not approve?'

To his surprise, she laughed with evident enjoyment.

'You are absurd! It is positively of no use to try and tease me, because, you know, I have no less than six brothers about me at home!' She sobered, then added thoughtfully. 'But all the same, you have surprised me.'

He gave a theatrical sigh. 'And I suppose it's not of the slightest use to ask you why. You are shockingly bad at answering questions. I wonder they did not beat you at school.

But I suppose that rarely happens at girls' schools — a pity, one sometimes feels.'

'Well, it certainly didn't happen at the Misses More's school, thank goodness,' said Alethea. 'And I propose to ignore your final comment, sir!'

'As you ignore most of my questions,' he pointed out, flourishing the whip at her. 'Now, pray don't be so provoking! Do tell me why you said I had surprised you.'

She was feeling decidedly more in charity with him now, so she did not hesitate. 'Oh, because you were teasing me,' she admitted. 'Somehow I did not connect you with anything of the kind. Not in a kindly way, that is —' she broke off, conscious of having made a blunder.

He raised one eyebrow, a pained expression on his face. 'Egad! She thinks me a very monster — no wonder she didn't wish to drive out with me today, or any day, come to that! I am shocked, madam, shocked to the core that you should hold such a wretched opinion of me.'

'More of your nonsense,' she said, smiling a little shamefacedly, for she realised that her tongue had outrun her civility. 'But in excuse I must urge that — as I said before — I do not know you very well.'

'Then we must remedy that,' he said, promptly. 'I can no longer endure to leave you in any doubt as to the true amiability — not to say nobility — of my disposition. It shall be my earnest endeavour from this day forward to see that you are afforded every opportunity of studying my character at first hand. I have observed already that you are a keen student of human nature. And you may as well have a willing subject on which to exercise your talents, don't you agree, ma'am?'

She felt all her antagonism towards him ebbing away, and her grey eyes were dancing as she raised her face to his. 'It certainly seems a reasonable supposition,' she agreed, demurely.

'Then you will drive out with me again tomorrow?' he pleaded.

She was quite surprised how difficult it was to refuse, but prudence won. 'Thank you, but I have a previous engagement.'

'Then possibly on Monday?' he persisted.

'I'm sorry, but we are to go to the play that evening and dine with the Fothergills. There would not be time.'

'But at this rate,' he protested, in his usual drawl, 'we shall never contrive to become better acquainted. Egad, I see I must carry you off by force — there's nothing else for it.'

She was still laughing at this outrageous statement when a vehicle approaching from the other direction pulled up beside them. Glancing across at it, they saw Vivyan Allerton with Lydia seated beside him, her eyes wide in astonishment.

'Gracious, is it you, Alethea?' she asked, in a shrill tone. 'Well, this *is* a surprise, to be sure!'

Alethea quite expected a display of temperament on Lydia's part once they were alone again indoors, but to her surprise little was said.

'So Beau Devenish took pity on you, did he?' remarked her cousin. 'Well, I hope you won't be refining too much upon that, because I've already warned you how it is with him.'

'You need have no alarms on my account,' replied Alethea carelessly.

'I dare say, but for all that he's prodigiously attractive! And you wouldn't be the first female by any means who had meant to keep a cool head, and ended by becoming hopelessly infatuated.'

'Sir James Devenish is not at all the kind of man who has the power to raise the slightest interest in me.'

'Who is, then, I wonder?' mocked Lydia. 'I suppose you'll say you find your staid poet more to your liking? He is the greatest bore in nature, and not to be compared to Devenish in any way!'

'One can only be thankful for that,' retorted Alethea, drily. 'But I wish, Lydia, you would rid yourself of the notion that I am set on attaching myself to some gentleman or other. Nothing is further from my thoughts, I assure you.'

'Ay, so you say, but I think it a great piece of nonsense, cousin. However, we have said all this before, and I am not in the mood for argument.'

'Did you have a pleasant drive with Mr Allerton?' asked Alethea, glad to turn the subject.

Lydia's face glowed. 'Oh, delightful! I feared, you know, that he was taking too much for granted after yesterday, and that I might have trouble with him. But he was so gay and amusing, exactly in the way that Devenish is, and though his *looks* told me he admired me, he didn't utter one single embarrassing word. I think,' she added, flippantly, 'that I shall make him my new flirt — one must have someone, and I am quite tired of Devenish, who never means anything.'

'Is that quite fair?' asked Alethea, before she could stop herself.

'Fair?' Lydia stared, then laughed, 'All's fair in love and war, don't they say?'

Alethea shrugged, tired of the conversation, and picked up a book. It was none of her business, but she could not help feeling some qualms for Vivyan Allerton. His feelings for Lydia obviously went deeper than the ready admiration she aroused in most men; and although Lydia herself could evidently see this, she was still not prepared to spare him.

The two went driving together again on the following day, Lydia looking charming in a russet riding dress and jaunty feathered hat to match. She had kept Allerton waiting almost half an hour while she put the finishing touches to this costume; but he betrayed no impatience, in the meantime chatting amiably to Mrs Manbury and Alethea in the parlour. As he rose to greet his dilatory passenger, Alethea noticed the glad light that sprang to his eyes. She looked quickly away, embarrassed. It was altogether too bad of Lydia.

She herself spent a pleasant afternoon with the two Allerton girls, although the arrangement had been made hurriedly after she had told Devenish of a previous engagement for today. She wished to make quite certain that, if he should call, he would find her from home. She was uncertain what caprice could have made him call to take her out yesterday, but she had no intention of allowing it to be repeated. Let him play his sophisticated games with someone who could enjoy them. According to Lydia, there must be plenty of candidates.

Chapter XI

Alethea had been looking forward to her visit to the theatre, but her enjoyment was somewhat overcast by the dinner party at Caroline's which preceded it. Lydia's sister seemed in a particularly scratchy mood, continually arguing over trivialities with her husband, who did his best to placate her by turning the other cheek. Alethea reflected impatiently that, although this was no doubt exemplary conduct for a host, it was obviously the worst way of dealing with Caroline. Every soft answer seemed to inflame her bitterness and increase her bickering. A sharp retort, if bad manners on his part, might have reminded his wife of what was due to her guests.

Lydia and Allerton seemed unaffected by this display of matrimonial disharmony. For the most part, they were completely absorbed in their own conversation, which seemed to be affording Lydia a great deal of amusement. Allerton did not laugh nearly so often, but his expression radiated pleasure. Evidently he was bent on entertaining his partner, and succeeding in spite of the uncongenial atmosphere surrounding them.

Unfortunately, Mr Tracy was unable to throw off the effects of his surroundings in the same way. A shy man at best, he became more awkward and tongue-tied than usual, even though Alethea tried her hardest to initiate conversations on literary topics likely to interest him. He simply answered her in monosyllables and stared down at his plate; one might have thought that he found food the most interesting object in the room, but for the fact that he ate very little.

For some members of the party, at any rate, it was a welcome relief when the meal at last came to an end and they all set out for the theatre. Once they entered the box, Alethea speedily forgot all that had gone before in her eager anticipation of what was to come. She paid scant heed to her cousins, who kept craning over the side to scan the audience and exclaim whenever they recognised someone.

'There is Sheridan in the next box with the Linley family,' Caroline informed them, scarcely troubling to lower her voice. 'Oh, and look, Lydia! Devenish is over there, with Calver, and some others whom I don't know — yes, they've seen us.'

She broke off for a moment to acknowledge the bows from a box opposite before beginning her commentary afresh.

'Devenish acquiring a little culture, eh?' asked Allerton, with a laugh. 'That's a new start, egad!'

'But everyone comes to see Mrs Siddons,' said Lydia. 'She's quite the latest craze.'

'Well, Devenish usually likes to make the fashions, not follow 'em. I'll wager he's got other reasons for being here tonight than watching the Divine Sarah perform,' replied Allerton, knowingly.

'For shame, Vivyan!' Lydia dimpled at him. 'I dare say you judge the poor creature by yourself. Tell me, do you have other reasons for being here?'

For a moment his eyes rested on her bewitching face with an intense look which made her catch her breath. Then he looked away, laughed, and answered her in a light tone.

'One reason only, but a very good reason.'

She was too accomplished a flirt to let this pass. 'Oh, but I must know it — I am beyond anything curious! Do, pray, tell me!'

'I think you know it already,' he said, keeping his glance turned away from her provocative smile. 'But see, the curtain is rising.'

There was a momentary hush as the curtains swished back revealing the stage; but the chatter soon broke out again, though not quite so loudly as before. Alethea turned to Paul Tracy with a gesture of annoyance. Playgoing was an infrequent pleasure in her life, and she wanted to become completely immersed in the play from the very start, not to be distracted by a chattering audience. His answering look showed her that he sympathised with this view. She felt vaguely comforted; since coming to London, she had found few people to share any of her preferences or opinions.

But when Sarah Siddons herself appeared on stage, the silence was such that even Alethea and Mr Tracy could approve. Although the actress was not much above middle height, she seemed to dominate the scene. She had strong rather than beautiful features, with a particularly brilliant eye and a mobile expression, and her hair was red. Her movements, though graceful, were never languid, but performed with the energy required by her part. But it was her voice which carried the audience with her, spellbound; a voice which ranged through all the emotions from tender melancholy to impassioned fervour.

The play was an old favourite by Southerne entitled *Isabella or The Fatal Marriage*, and it gave full scope for the pathos and emotion which the actress was so well able to convey. The plot concerned a poverty-stricken widow who re-married to provide security for her child, only to discover afterwards that her previous husband was still living. The emotional impact of the play was considerably heightened by the fact that the part of the child was being played by Mrs Siddons's own eight-year-old son, Henry.

The first act ended with an awed hush from the audience. Then shouts and plaudits began to ring out, and it was some time before people started to move from their seats to stretch their legs before the second act began.

Alethea and Mr Tracy strolled out with the rest, deep in discussion of the play. They were both so absorbed in their conversation that they barely interrupted it to respond to the greetings of Beau Devenish and Lord Calver, who had come over to join their party.

Devenish moved over to Allerton's side, as Lydia's attention was caught by someone else for a moment.

'Who the devil is that fellow?' he asked.

'What fellow? Oh, Tracy, you mean. You've just been presented to him this minute, my dear chap.'

'I know his name, yes,' drawled Devenish. 'But what is he, and how does Miss Newnham come to be so very thick with him?'

'According to Lydia, they met at one of these Bluestocking Soirees of Mrs Montagu's that Miss Newnham attended,' replied Allerton in an undertone. 'Fellow's a poet, I collect — would you believe it? Curst rum customers they get at those gatherings, by all accounts! Wouldn't catch me going there at any price, give you my word.'

'A poet, eh? I've never heard of him.'

'No, well, hardly likely you would, old fellow, now is it? I've yet to learn that you're a keen student of literature, what?'

'It may be, dear boy, that you have much to learn about me,' reproved Devenish, taking a pinch of snuff and eyeing Paul Tracy intently under cover of the manoeuvre. 'What kind of chap is he, would you say? You've spent most of the evening in his company, so you must have some idea. I must say he don't look one to set the Thames afire.'

'That he's not,' replied Allerton, with a laugh. 'Stuffy, that's how I'd sum him up — when he's not positively tongue-tied, that's to say.'

'Which he's certainly not at present,' said Devenish, watching Alethea's animated expression as she listened to something Tracy was saying.

'Oh, well, Miss Newnham understands his kind of conversation. They seem to go on famously. But, I say, James, did you ever see anything like that coat the fellow's wearing? I ask you!'

'Not since I was breeched, certainly. Seem to think that style was high fashion then. Still, the chap must have something to make Miss Newnham hang on his every word.'

Allerton stared, then chuckled. 'I say, can it be that you're *jealous*, old fellow? I'd no notion the girl meant so much to you, must say!'

'What she means to me,' said Devenish, languidly, 'is that she's a quarry who seems to be eluding my grasp. And that, you know —' he shook his head solemnly — 'is something we can't have. No, decidedly not. Instincts of the chase, and all that.'

'Seems to me —' began Allerton, then stopped. Devenish raised an inquiring eyebrow. 'Well, must you?' went on the other, slightly on the defensive. 'Mean to say — she's a nice girl, a sincere girl, and not really up to snuff. Intelligent as they come, oh, yes, but not quite versed in the ways of the Town. She might — well, she might get hurt,' he finished, quickly, reddening a trifle under Devenish's mocking gaze.

'You've been seeing a good deal of the fair Lydia lately,' remarked Devenish, by way of reply.

'Yes. Have you any objection?'

'Not the least in the world, for myself.'

'What d'you mean?' asked Allerton, quickly.

'Only —' Devenish paused to flick a speck of dust from his sleeve — 'only that perhaps I, too, dislike seeing people get hurt.'

Allerton did not answer for a moment; then he said jerkily, 'I thought perhaps — if I didn't rush things —'

Devenish shook his head. 'They mean her for Bedwyn,' he said gently.

'Bedwyn! Good God, you can't mean that! Of all the infamous —'

At this point they were interrupted by the others, and soon they all resumed their places for the second act. During the rest of the play, the audience sat spellbound while Mrs Siddons played upon their emotions with such consummate artistry that as the curtain fell, there was scarcely a dry eye in the house. Caroline, making copious use of her own handkerchief, drew the attention of the others to the next box, where Sheridan was standing to applaud, the tears streaming freely down his face.

When they at last emerged from the theatre to seek their carriages, the three girls were shivering a little; though whether from exposure to the night air or to their recent emotional experience, none of them could determine.

Chapter XII

During the week that followed, Vivyan Allerton contrived to see Lydia almost every day. She had too much prudence to permit him to take her out driving as frequently as he would have wished, so he had to fall back on such devices as persuading his mother and sisters to pay more than their usual number of calls on the Manburys. He racked his wits endlessly to hatch schemes which would throw him into her company, and eventually came up with a suggestion that they should all attend a masquerade to be held at the Pantheon on the following Friday.

When the Pantheon was first opened about twelve years previously, Horace Walpole had described it as 'a new winter Ranelagh in Oxford Road — the most elegant edifice in England.' Assemblies, balls, concerts and masquerades were regularly held there for subscribers, who were for the most part, people of fashion. An attempt was made to exclude the gay ladies of the town and other undesirable elements; but, as subscribers could take what friends they pleased, this was not always successful. Nevertheless, there was nothing at that time in the Pantheon's reputation to cause Mrs Manbury to object to the inclusion of her daughter and niece in the Allertons' party, once she was assured that one of Vivyan's married sisters would be present.

'If Mama fancies that Jane Mervyn will make a good chaperone,' laughed Lydia, once the two girls were alone, 'she could not be more mistaken! Why, Jane's but nine and twenty, and more giddy by half than my sister Caroline! Though to do Caro justice, she's never a spoilsport, and knows well enough how to look the other way when needful. Nor does she go carrying tales to Mama afterwards.'

'I should hope not!' exclaimed Alethea in horror. Having been brought up in an all-male household, she had been taught from a very early age to view tale-bearing with disgust.

'Well, lots of sisters do,' rejoined Lydia. 'My sister Eleanor was a perfect cat when she was at home! It was for ever "Mama, Lydia's done this" and "Mama, Lydia's done that", until there was no bearing it! We used to have some rare set-to's at times, I can tell you!'

'Well, families usually quarrel among themselves, but they close the ranks when an outsider joins in, don't they?'

Lydia nodded. 'The Allertons don't, though — quarrel, I mean. They're prodigiously good tempered people — I doubt if even the most cross grained person could force one of them to a quarrel!'

'Not even Mr Allerton?' asked Alethea. 'Men are often more quick to anger than females.'

'Vivyan, do you mean?' Alethea nodded. 'Why, Vivyan is the kindest, sweetest tempered soul alive!' continued Lydia, in a rush. 'He's so different from every other man I've met — I do believe I could twist him around my little finger!'

'You seem to be able to do that with most men, as far as I can see,' said Alethea.

'Oh, yes, if you mean that most of them like to flirt with me, and such like nonsense,' agreed Lydia, in a straightforward acceptance of fact which did not sound at all conceited. 'But it's altogether different with Viv. He —'

She broke off and an unusually gentle look came into her eyes, so that for the first time Alethea found herself warming towards this spoilt child who was her cousin.

'Vivyan really means it, you see,' Lydia went on in a wondering tone. 'It isn't just that he's dazzled by me, or wishes to own me as a desirable piece of property, or to cut someone else out for the sport of the thing. He really and truly *cares* for me, Alethea — I believe he would even if I were as plain as — as Melissa Woodthorpe! And although you haven't met her yet, Alethea, I assure you she has a face and figure like a pudding, not to mention a slight squint!'

Alethea nodded. 'And what of you, Lydia? How do you feel towards Mr Allerton?'

Lydia started to speak, coloured a little, then choked back the words and bounced out of her chair.

'Oh, pray come along, Cousin! We can't dawdle here all day talking, you know! We have to visit Madame Delice to see about our ball gowns, for one thing. By the way, do you think we should go to the Masquerade in costume, or in dominoes and masks? I have a fancy to go attired as a Turkish dancing girl — what do you think? Would Mama allow it, do you suppose?'

Alethea knew quite well that her Aunt would instantly veto such a scheme, but she did not trouble herself to say so. Lydia's mind was obviously not at all on what she was saying; she was talking to drown her own thoughts. She continued to be vague and abstracted during their visit to the modiste's, actually answering 'Yes' when asked whether she would prefer a ruched frill or lace as an edging to the sleeves of her gown. Mrs Manbury called her sharply to order, and eventually all the details were settled. The gowns were promised for three days before the date of Alethea's ball, which had been fixed for Thursday of the week following.

'Everybody has accepted,' Mrs Manbury informed them as the carriage rattled homewards over the cobbles. 'I've heard from Bedwyn, too, Lydia, and he will be present.'

There was a sudden silence in the carriage. Alethea stole a look at her cousin, and saw a strained expression on her face.

'Well?' Mrs Manbury's tone was sharp. 'Haven't you anything to say?'

Lydia passed a hand across her forehead. 'Oh, yes, Mama, of course — but I've such a headache come on, I can't think properly.'

'I thought you were quiet at Madame Delice's. I dare say it's all that racketing about in Vivyan's carriage. It will have to stop when Bedwyn returns to town, Lydia, if he isn't to take the wrong notion. Of course, everyone else knows that you and Vivyan are practically brother and sister, and for him to drive you around is a deal less likely to cause tongues to wag than when you used to go with Devenish. Not that,' she finished, 'anyone is fool enough to take *his* attentions seriously; only as I've said to you before, it does tend to keep others away. A girl needs to weigh all these considerations very carefully if she's to make a good match.'

'Oh, Mama, pray don't nag! You've said all this before a dozen times, until I am quite tired of it!' snapped Lydia.

Mrs Manbury subsided, making allowance for her daughter's headache, and peace was preserved for the rest of the journey.

When they reached home, they found that Mr Tracy had called in their absence, leaving a book for Alethea. She examined the fly leaf and saw that it was a volume of his own poems. A slip of paper fluttered from its pages to the floor. She picked it up and read the few lines it contained.

It is with some reluctance that I leave this for your perusal, conscious as I am of its many faults. It is yours, if perchance you should wish to own it once you have read my poor verses.

Do you go to Mrs Montagu's soiree tomorrow se'ennight? In the hope of meeting you there —

I am, dear madam,
Your very obliged servant,
Paul Tracy.

'Another book!' exclaimed Lydia. ''Pon rep, Alethea, you have as little need as anyone to depend upon the Circulating Library! I collect from its size that this is a volume of poetry?'

Alethea nodded. 'Mr Tracy's own poems. I was asking him about his own work when we were at Drury Lane together.'

'I suppose,' said Mrs Manbury, doubtfully, 'that there is nothing in it that a young girl should not — but no, I am convinced that Mr Tracy is not the man to offer you anything that is not perfectly proper for you to read.'

Alethea could not resist rising to this. 'And what precisely would you say is *improper* for one to read, Aunt?'

'You must know perfectly well what I mean, child. I have never been a great reader of poetry, but from what little I recall, it seems to me that too often poets treat of sordid subjects, or else couch their verse in language that can only be considered too — too outspoken for a delicate female mind.'

'Well, mercifully mine is not a delicate female mind — or, at least, not to that extent,' retorted Alethea, with energy. 'One must surely not expect a literary work always to keep to the elegant language of the drawing room! If so, then no schoolgirl could ever be trusted with the classics, many parts of Shakespeare's works, or, indeed, even the Bible.'

Mrs Manbury compressed her lips. 'You have had an unusual upbringing, Alethea, and therefore you may see matters differently from some of us. It may be all very well to air such opinions among your own family; but if you will heed a word of advice from me — and, after all, your Mama placed you in my charge — you will not be as free with them before strangers.'

Alethea choked back the reply which hovered on her lips, and said instead 'Very well, Aunt Olivia. I am sorry if I should have said anything to vex you. Such was not my intention.'

Mrs Manbury inclined her head in acknowledgement of the apology, feeling thankful that Lydia, at any rate, did not entertain such odd notions as her cousin's. How in the world was she ever to find a husband for the girl? Certainly this Mr Tracy must be given every possible encouragement, for who else was likely to consider such an arrant bluestocking for a wife? All the same, it was a pity; a girl with Alethea's looks (though not to be compared to Lydia's, of course) and her more than respectable fortune, might have easily set her sights higher than an insignificant, somewhat dowdy minor poet. There was some consolation, reflected Mrs Manbury, in the fact that so far Alethea had met very few people at all. Things might improve after the ball in her honour had brought her a wider acquaintance. Neither had she passed completely unnoticed by the few eligible gentlemen whom she had met up to the present time. Even Beau Devenish had thought it worth his while to take her out in his phaeton on one occasion, even if it had obviously been in substitution for Lydia. True, he had not repeated the experiment; and no wonder, thought Mrs Manbury indignantly, if Alethea had played off some of her airs against him. But he had called in with Vivyan Allerton a few days later, and shown a mild disposition to try and get up a tentative flirtation with Alethea while Lydia was being so very charming to Vivyan.

As might have been expected, Alethea had not given him the smallest encouragement, so that presently he had recollected another engagement, and taken his leave. At this stage in her thoughts, Mrs Manbury recollected in time that she did not wish Alethea — or either of the girls, for that matter — to encourage Beau Devenish in a flirtation; indeed, she had specifically warned them against that very thing. Illogically, she still felt annoyed with her niece, and more than ever determined that she would see the girl engaged to someone before the season was ended, if it should be the last thing she was able to accomplish.

With her usual perception, Alethea guessed most of what was passing in her Aunt's mind, but it did not disturb her unduly. She had come to accept the fact that their ideas were poles apart, and she had more important claims on her attention at that moment — Paul Tracy's reference to the soiree at Mrs Montagu's, for instance. It would be splendid to go there again, but how was this to be accomplished? After a pause for thought, she asked her aunt if it might be possible for them to pay a call on Miss More at Hampton.

Mrs Manbury assented a trifle grudgingly. 'When do you wish to go?'

'Oh, as soon as may be. Would tomorrow be convenient?' asked Alethea, diffidently.

After a little discussion, it was decided that the following morning would do very well. 'A short drive into the country may be no bad thing in this lovely weather,' said Mrs Manbury, warming to the plan. 'But, mind, Alethea, I don't intend to make it a lengthy visit — half an hour at the most. Longer I cannot engage for, as I find Miss More one of the most difficult creatures in the world to converse with, I assure you!'

Glad to have gained her Aunt's consent, Alethea let this criticism pass.

'We will start immediately after breakfast, should the day be fine,' started Mrs Manbury. 'And on our way back, Lydia, we might find time to buy some gloves to match your new ball gown.'

'Oh, no, Mama, I shan't be coming with you. I have a score of other things I must do.'

'What other things?' demanded her mother.

'Oh, I don't know — letter to write, and — and — oh, a multitude of things!'

Mrs Manbury capitulated. She could not blame Lydia in the slightest for evading a visit to Miss Hannah More. Only Alethea detected a false note in her cousin's voice, and wondered what exactly Lydia had in mind for tomorrow. Still, it was no concern of hers.

The visit was paid, and Alethea returned from it in high spirits. Miss More had undertaken to accompany her to the soirée on Tuesday. It seemed that Mrs Montagu had mentioned particularly how pleased she would be to see Miss Newnham again at her house in Portman Square. Mrs Manbury gave her consent, but Alethea could see that her Aunt thought she must be mad to take pleasure in an evening without music, cards or dancing to while away the hours.

'I declare it would soon set me nodding,' Mrs Manbury said with a laugh. 'However, you'll have dancing enough at your ball a few days afterwards. I have asked Mr Tracy, you know, and he has accepted. I fear it may be a sad crush, but that's better than being too thin of company, after all.'

Alethea nodded, her spirits temporarily overcast. She did not find as much pleasure in the prospect of this ball as she felt she ought, considering the trouble her Aunt was taking over it. Her experience of such affairs was small, being limited to impromptu dances held in neighbouring houses at home in Somerset; apart from one Assembly ball in Bristol to which she had been escorted by her brother Harry and a group of family friends. She would know so few people at her Aunt's ball, and those few were only recent acquaintances. Not that she found it at all difficult to make new acquaintances; but one always enjoyed oneself best among old friends.

They reached home somewhat earlier than might have been expected, and went straight to the parlour to tell Lydia that they were back. Mrs Manbury was smiling as she opened the door, but the smile froze on her lips when she saw the two occupants of the room.

It was Lydia and Vivyan Allerton, sitting quite alone and very close together.

Chapter XIII

Allerton rose at once to make his bow, but there was no mistaking the coldness of Mrs Manbury's greeting, in marked contrast to her usual way of speaking to him. Her face was like a thundercloud. After a few polite attempts at conversation which were icily repulsed, he took his leave with a slightly hangdog air.

No sooner had the door closed upon him than the storm burst.

'What can you mean, Miss, by receiving a gentleman when you are alone in the house, and sitting with him in that *intimate* way?' demanded Mrs Manbury, in a towering passion. 'Are you quite lost to all sense of propriety and prudence? Only wait until your father learns of this — as he shall do, I give you my word, the moment he sets foot in the house!'

Alethea could not help thinking that her poor uncle was in for a wretched homecoming, and that could he but know of it, he would most likely go to his Club instead.

Lydia for once looked both contrite and frightened. 'It was nothing, Mama, truly — the merest accident! He hadn't been here much above ten minutes — I swear it!'

'Then that was ten minutes too long! But I don't need to tell you that! What could you be thinking of to have him admitted to the house *at all* in my absence, or unless your cousin had been here, at least, to preserve the proprieties? You know better than this, my girl, and we'll see if your father can improve the lesson you seem to have forgot! Never in all my life —'

'Mama, it was not either of our faults, truly it wasn't.' Lydia was sobbing now. 'The footman didn't say you were from home, he just showed him in — Vivyan was as surprised as I was — he stood there for a moment — then — then — he had something to tell me about the arrangements for — for — the Masquerade —' she produced the word with a gulp — 'and it seemed s-silly not to say it, since — since he was there —'

Mrs Manbury's unnaturally high colour subsided a little. 'I'll speak to Dawkins,' she said, ominously. 'Anyway, you should have told Vivyan to come back later, and had him shown out at once. Don't you realise how servants gossip, foolish girl? Suppose this should come to Bedwyn's ears, especially if he should also learn how much you and Allerton have been seeing of each other lately! It should well put him off!'

'I don't care if it does,' muttered Lydia mutinously, drying her eyes with the handkerchief which Alethea had passed to her after she had failed to find her own. 'I'm sick of hearing Bedwyn's name — sick, I tell you!'

She threw back her head, prepared to go into a fit of hysterics, but Mrs Manbury was too quick for her. A sharp slap on the face brought Lydia to her senses. With one hand nursing the rapidly reddening cheek, she sat still, glowering at her mother.

'You will go to your room,' ordered Mrs Manbury, in icy accents, 'and you will remain there until you have come to a more sensible frame of mind. As for this Masquerade at the Pantheon,' she continued, as Lydia rose sullenly to do her bidding, 'you can put that scheme entirely out of your head. I shall not allow you to go, now.'

'Oh, no, Mama, you couldn't be so unjust!' Lydia burst into tears again. 'It's all settled — and — and — Alethea was so looking forward to it —'

Mrs Manbury switched her eyes from daughter to niece. 'I certainly am surprised to hear that,' she said coldly. 'I had the impression that your cousin did not mind very much whether she went or not. But there's no reason why *she* should not, if indeed she's set her heart on it.'

Alethea shook her head. She was embarrassed by the scene between mother and daughter, which she felt was none of her business. She had been wanting for some time to leave them alone, but feared that if she walked out, it might give offence to her Aunt and only make things worse for Lydia.

'I wouldn't wish to go without Lydia,' she said, in a mild tone.

'Then that is settled!' snapped Mrs Manbury. 'Lydia — upstairs, out of my sight, until you've come to your senses! And pray control yourself, as we don't want the servants nosing it abroad that you and I have quarrelled on account of this morning's work. Their tongues will be busy enough already, I'll warrant!'

Lydia wiped her eyes furiously with Alethea's handkerchief and rushed from the room, choking down her sobs. After a moment, Alethea excused herself to her Aunt and followed her cousin upstairs. She reached the head of the staircase in time to hear the slam of Lydia's door. She hesitated a moment before going into her own room. It would do no good to go to Lydia yet. She took up the volume of Paul Tracy's poetry, and tried to concentrate on it.

About a quarter of an hour later, she heard a quiet knock on her door. Opening it she saw Lydia on the threshold. She was looking more like herself, but still distressed. Alethea drew her gently inside, closing the door quietly behind her.

'Oh, Alethea, what am I to do? I can't bear it if Papa finds out — he may speak to Vivyan! And then Vivyan will feel obliged to offer for me, and then — oh, everything will be so complicated, I can't think what will happen! You must tell me

107

what to do — you're so calm and always have your wits about you! And I *must* go to the Pantheon Masquerade — I must! What can I possibly say in excuse for *not* going, when it's all settled, and the whole Allerton family knows about it? They must think it very strange that Mama should suddenly forbid it, after agreeing only the other day. Oh, what can I do? She is so unreasonable — so cruel! I detest her!'

'Hush, you mustn't put yourself in a taking,' said Alethea, soothingly, putting an arm about her cousin and guiding her to a chair. 'There, sit down, and let's discuss things quietly.'

'Mama is a beast!' Lydia said, vehemently.

'Well, I'll agree she was very hard on you. But, all the same, Lydia, you did ask for trouble in letting Mr Allerton remain when you were alone. I can quite see how it might have come about, but why didn't you send him off at once? He, too, must have realised he oughtn't to stay, surely?'

'Well, for one thing I didn't expect Mama to be returning quite so soon,' replied Lydia, ingenuously. 'And for another — oh, I don't know! He had things to tell me, and we got talking, and then the time just seemed to fly, and I forgot all about the proprieties — and everything else of the kind —'

'But I thought you said he was with you for only ten minutes?'

'Oh, it seemed like ten minutes, anyway,' said Lydia airily. 'I don't know how long it may have been. But what does any of that matter now? Papa will be vexed, and I shall miss the Masquerade, and heaven above knows what mischief may come of it all! I am quite distracted, Alethea, truly I am! Can you not think of something to do?'

Alethea pondered for a moment. 'I would say the best thing is for you to have another talk with my Aunt — an unemotional one, this time. She must be as alive as you are to the possible consequences of telling your father about this, and I know she's every bit as concerned to avoid them. I don't think it would be too difficult for you to persuade her to drop that part of the — punishment, I suppose we must call it. As for the visit to the Pantheon, well, that might be more difficult. You may have to give in about that, and concentrate instead on finding an excuse that won't sound too thin to the Allertons, for our not being able to go.'

'I am determined to go!' stormed Lydia. 'I shall go whether Mama forbid it or not, see if I don't!'

Alethea shook her head. 'It's of no use, my dear. You'll ruin everything if you work yourself up into a passion. I don't know my Aunt as well as you do, of course; but from the little I do know, I would say that reason would influence her more than a display of histrionics.'

Lydia nodded, thoughtful now. 'You're quite right. Mama's not really an emotional female at all — I've rarely seen her as heated as she was just now. Her anger's more the cold kind, that withers one.' She rose from the chair and walked over to Alethea's dressing table, where she surveyed herself critically in the mirror. 'I'll go and tidy myself — I look a fright! And then I'll do as you say, Alethea. You won't mind, will you, keeping out of the way for a while? Until I've had my talk with Mama, I mean. I'll come up and tell you how it goes.'

Alethea agreed, and her cousin went towards the door. With one hand on the knob, she turned and gave the other girl a quick, sincere smile.

'And thank you, Alethea. Do you know, I didn't like you above half until this minute, but now I feel perhaps we can be friends, after all.'

'I do hope so. Now make haste; and don't forget to let me know when I may come downstairs, or I shall moulder away here for years, like some poor hermit in his cell.'

Lydia had quite a cool head of her own, and she recognised the wisdom of her cousin's advice. After having made herself presentable, therefore, she went downstairs in search of her mother, determined to use all her powers of persuasion, but to keep calm whatever the outcome might be.

She carried her first point with unexpected ease. Mrs Manbury agreed not to tell her husband about his daughter's lapse from grace. The fact was that she had now had time to think the matter over, and had come to the same conclusion as Lydia. It was increasingly obvious that the Allerton boy, as she thought of him, was head over heels in love with Lydia and would soon be making a formal declaration. He must be headed off until they knew for certain what the Duke of Bedwyn's intentions were; if Bedwyn failed to come up to scratch, then possibly Vivyan might be considered. Lord Calver would have been a better match, of course, but unfortunately he did seem to be rather taken with Felicia Allerton. Not that a determined effort on Lydia's part — but that could all be worked out more carefully later. The immediate concern must be to keep Vivyan Allerton at arm's length for the moment; and if Lydia's father knew of this morning's indiscretion, he would most likely consider it his duty to speak to Vivyan, thus precipitating an offer of marriage.

She repeated all this to her daughter, and Lydia agreed. So far, all, was harmony. But when the proposed visit to the Pantheon was mentioned, she was firmly in opposition.

'There has been quite enough nonsense between you, and I think you must make up your mind to see far less of Vivyan than you've fallen into the way of doing just lately.'

'But, Mama, you said it couldn't signify, as we had been childhood playmates, and our family always so close to the Allertons,' protested Lydia.

'Yes, I know I did, but I've changed my mind. Something Margaret Nayland said to me the other day set me thinking how it must look to outsiders — and once people notice anything of the kind, it's not long before gossip spreads. You know well enough how such rumours get about, and we've neither of us any wish to have Bedwyn frightened off by them.'

For a moment, Lydia almost forgot her resolution not to argue with her mother. She choked back the heated words, and forced herself to answer calmly.

'But, Mama, it's all arranged — the Allertons must think it so odd if I say now that I'm not going! What possible excuse can I give, when only this morning Vivyan and I were discussing it as quite settled?'

'I've thought of that,' replied Mrs Manbury, triumphantly, 'and I have an excellent excuse ready for you. Eleanor wrote yesterday to say she would like you and Alethea to go and stay there for a few days, if you can possibly spare the time from your other engagements. She's feeling a bit moped at present, naturally enough, for she can't get about a great deal now, with only a month to go before her confinement. I had meant to suggest that you might go there for a few days after Alethea's ball is over, but there is no reason why you cannot go at once, tomorrow. I can send a message over with one of the grooms today, and I know it will delight your sister to see you so soon. What better excuse can there be than this? You have only to say that she positively insists on seeing you at once. No one will think to question the whims of a female who is breeding.'

Chapter XIV

Lydia's face took on a mutinous look.

'Go to Eleanor's?' she exclaimed, in outraged tones, all her good resolutions forgotten. 'To that wretched house in the depths of the country! Mama, you know quite well how I detest the country! And pray what should we find to do at Harrow, especially with Eleanor in her present condition?'

'There is a pleasant park at Roxeth Place for you to walk in. The country air will do you good.'

'I don't wish to be done good to! I shall be just as moped to death as you say Eleanor feels, after I've been there a day or two!'

'Nonsense,' replied her mother, briskly. 'Harrow is not precisely a desert — there's always plenty going on there. Your sister has neighbours who will be calling on her, inviting you to dinner parties and the like. Devenish's grandmother, Lady Carteret, for instance, lives quite close, and Eleanor says she calls frequently. I understand she is very fond of a game of whist.'

'Devenish's grandmother!' repeated Lydia, in stupefied accents. 'A game of whist! Lud, Mama, what do you take me for? Such pastimes may suit Eleanor well enough in her present state of health, but I require something a little more stimulating, if I am to find my life even tolerable!'

'Nevertheless, you will go. I have quite made up my mind.' Mrs Manbury's tone was firm. 'A few days of early nights and fresh air will be no bad thing for you — we can't have you looking peaky for Bedwyn's return, you know, and London life does take its toll, there's no denying. I shall send a message to

Eleanor at once to expect you and your cousin tomorrow. Alethea has an engagement with Miss More for Tuesday evening, and then there is the ball on Thursday, so it can only be a short visit, but I know your sister will quite understand. You had best return on Monday — Sunday travel is not to be thought of, naturally, more especially as Alethea is a clergyman's daughter. Now, it's no use arguing with me, Lydia — I am quite determined. And you really have very little to complain of; four days in the country should not unduly tax even your small powers of endurance.'

Lydia wished very much to argue, but she knew from past experience that it was futile once her mother's mind was set on a course. Compressing her lips to keep back the rebellious words, she went upstairs to acquaint Alethea with what was in store for them both.

On her side, Alethea had no very strong objection to the plan. The Masquerade would have been a new experience for her, and she liked new experiences; but her heart was not set on it. Moreover, she welcomed the thought of a few days out of London in this sudden heat of early June. Having been born and bred in the country, she felt she could face with equanimity the rigours of a short sojourn in rural Middlesex. So although she listened sympathetically enough while Lydia vented her feelings for a while, she did not share her cousin's dismay.

'I dare say it will not be so bad as you think,' she said, consolingly. 'And no doubt you will be able to attend a Masquerade at the Pantheon at some other time. Let's make up our minds to enjoy our visit to your sister, if only for her sake.'

But Lydia refused to be comforted. Mrs Manbury announced her intention of calling on the Allertons straight away to explain how matters stood, but said she thought it would be best if she went alone.

'One look at your sulky face, miss,' she said tartly to Lydia, 'and they would know at once that you do not go willingly to visit Eleanor! I prefer that they should give you credit — however undeserved it may be — for some sisterly feeling.'

This the Allerton girls did, saying again and again how good natured it was of Lydia to give up the proposed outing to oblige her sister, and how very like her. Naturally, they were disappointed, but they quite understood. Vivyan's understanding was under some strain, but fortunately his manners were far too good to betray him into unguarded speech. He did venture to suggest to his sisters that they should wait until the next Masquerade at the Pantheon, when possibly Lydia and her cousin would be at liberty to join them; but there was an immediate outcry of protest at this.

'We've ordered our costumes, and everything!' complained Felicia. 'And Jane is so looking forward to it — she hasn't been to the Pantheon for an age! By all means let us take Lydia and Miss Newnham to the next one, but pray don't disappoint us for Friday, Viv, there's a dear.'

He was too good natured to withstand their pleas, but it was plain to see that for him all the attraction had gone out of the scheme.

'Oh, very well,' he said, with a laugh, 'since I don't doubt you'll nag me until I give in! But a nice thing it will be if it gets put about that I'm reduced to squiring my own sisters around nowadays.'

'You may escort *us* to the Pantheon,' retorted Felicia, in an aside, 'but I'll be bound we'll not see much of you once we're there. Some fair unknown or other will soon claim all your attention!'

Naturally Mrs Manbury did not hear this, but she faithfully reported everything else that had passed when she returned home. Lydia listened without comment, her mouth set in an obstinate line. Alethea hoped fervently that her cousin would soon recover from her tantrum, otherwise their visit would certainly be of little benefit to the unfortunate Eleanor.

That same evening, Vivyan Allerton looked in at White's Club in St James's and met Devenish there.

'Been playing too high?' Devenish asked him, raising his quizzing glass and subjecting his friend to a prolonged scrutiny. 'Got a touch of liver? Or could it be another organ that's affected? You look demmed blue-devilled, old fellow, give you my word.'

'Let be, James, I'm in no mood for your foolery,' replied Allerton, with a reluctant grin. 'I need a drink — will you join me, or are you for cards?'

'Presently. But in the meantime let's crack a bottle.' He signalled to a waiter, who speedily supplied their needs.

'Not a bad wine, this,' said Devenish, holding his glass up to the light, 'though not to be compared with some I sampled in Sussex a few days since. But doubtless that particular keg was not acquired through the usual channels. Such things happen in Sussex.'

'And what might you have been doing in Sussex?' asked Allerton, though without much interest.

'Since you are evidently all agog to know, I don't mind telling you that I was visiting a friend who wished to sell me a horse.'

'Any good?'

'Lamentable. I was forced to decline the offer. But not so lamentable, dear boy, if you don't mind my mentioning it, as your total lack of interest in my conversation.'

'I'm sorry James. I fear I *am* like a bear with a sore head tonight. Fact is —' he paused to drain his glass — 'I've something on my mind.'

Devenish leaned over to replenish the glass. 'That, as I believe I mentioned when we first met, is evident.' He hesitated, then said casually. 'Care to tell me about it?'

Allerton made no reply for a moment, but tipped half the contents of his glass down his throat in one gulp.

'Not ale, you know,' Devenish pointed out, gently. 'I agree it's only a tolerable wine, but still too good to swallow without tasting.'

'Hell and the devil, James! If you must know, I came here with the intention of —'

'Drowning your sorrows. Capital — we'll drown them together. But I might enter into the project with more fervour did I but know what your sorrows are. Not,' he added, languidly, 'that I have the least desire to pry into your concerns, my dear chap. If you don't wish to tell me, by all means let us talk of something else.'

'Don't want to talk of anything else — devil take it, I don't think I can — not tonight, at any rate,' muttered Allerton, a trifle incoherently. 'Of course I can tell you, James. We were at school together, weren't we? And at Oxford? Damme, if I could confide in you then, with all that went on in our salad days, I can confide in you now.'

'The motion is carried unanimously. And so?'

'I think you know, anyway. It's Lydia, of course.'

Devenish contented himself with a nod.

'I've been seeing a great deal of her lately,' Allerton went on. 'And she's seemed different somehow, almost as if —'

He broke off. Devenish looked at him gravely, for the moment all trace of raillery gone.

'Oh, you know how she generally is!' Allerton's tone was defensive. 'The men are always round her like flies round a honeypot, and she — well, one can't blame her if she rather enjoys being the centre of attraction, and is not altogether averse from a little harmless flirting with one and another. You yourself — well, of course, while you were dancing attendance on her, I didn't make any attempt to interfere. But since then, since we all went on that ridiculous sight-seeing tour, I've seen her almost every day. And I do think — though you may say I damned well flatter myself, and I can't blame you —' here he paused to finish off his wine with a gesture of bravado — 'I really do think that she's beginning to care for me a little.'

'If so, then there seems small cause for that gloomy face of yours,' commented Devenish, with a slight smile.

'You know better than that. It was you who told me that her parents intend her to marry Bedwyn — that doddering old man, old enough to be her grandfather, pretty near! — and though I could scarce credit it at the time, since then my mother's dropped a hint or two. And now it does look as though Mrs Manbury is trying to keep us apart. Lydia and her cousin were to join our party for the Masquerade at the Pantheon on Friday, but Mrs M. dropped in this morning to call off the arrangement. She'd got some demmed specious excuse about Lydia's married sister in Middlesex wanting some company for a day or two, but it didn't need Old Moore to see there was something other than that!' He looked at Devenish in appeal. 'What am I to do, James? I don't need to tell you I'm near crazed about Lydia — I dare say anyone could have seen it for this past year or more — and I fancy that at last I may be making some headway with her, however little. But it's too soon to declare myself; and now it looks as if I won't be given the chance to see her often enough to bring matters to a conclusion. I never felt so frustrated —' he brought his fist down on the table in a gesture which set the glasses and bottle dancing — 'in all my life! What in hell can I do about it? Answer me that!'

Devenish steadied the bottle in time to avert its collapse, and shook his head in gentle reproof. 'Not wash your coat in wine, Viv, at any rate. That would serve no purpose.'

Allerton looked puzzled for a moment. 'Wash my coat — oh, I see! I suppose it's too much to hope that you can ever be serious about anything?'

'Well, almost too much. For myself, dear fellow, I find that if life is to be tolerable, one must draw increasingly on one's sense of humour. To take things seriously is to admit a breach in one's defences.'

'That's your way of making sure you're not vulnerable — I know. I'm not as dense as you think, James.' Devenish made no answer. 'But I wish you could see your way to giving me some advice, for damned if I know what to do.'

'You could always follow the fair Lydia,' said Devenish, reflectively. 'Middlesex is not, after all, at the other end of the country. What part of Middlesex, by the way?'

For the first time, Allerton's face relaxed into a smile. 'A part we're all too familiar with, from our unregenerate youth.'

'You can't mean Harrow? Yes, I see you do. And now I come to think of it, I know quite well that Mrs Manbury's eldest daughter lives there. I've heard it from my grandmother — they're neighbours.'

'Are you suggesting —?'

'Why not? I really think it's high time that I paid a visit to my grandmother. She would like that extremely.'

Chapter XV

Roxeth Place, the country seat of Sir Roger Middleham, had been built for his father only twenty years previously, and presented a thoroughly modern appearance with its stucco exterior and pillared portico. Inside, all was comfort and good taste; decorations, furniture and hangings had all been renewed when Sir Roger took his bride there. Alethea, looking around her with an observant eye when she and Lydia first arrived, admired the cool, classical elegance of the principal rooms. She was particularly attracted by the drawing-room, which had several large windows giving views of well-laid out gardens, scattered here and there with classical statues. A marble temple stood beside an ornamental lake and beyond lay extensive parkland. She felt that, without any difficulty at all, she could pass a very pleasant few days in such surroundings.

Their welcome, too, was all that the most exacting visitor could have wished. Eleanor Middleham was delighted to see fresh faces about her; her husband greeted the newcomers with relief, as his wife's recent low spirits had tried his patience sorely. Now she was all animation, demanding news from Town and suggesting schemes for their entertainment while they were with her, scarcely pausing to hear their answers, or even to take a breath. Lydia, too, catching some of her sister's excitement, began to chatter animatedly, and her face lost its sulky look as she supplied Eleanor with the current tit-bits of gossip.

'I hear you are Devenish's latest flirt,' remarked Eleanor, with a twinkle.

'Oh, no, that's quite over now. He's amusing for a time, but one soon tires of his nonsense,' replied Lydia, carelessly.

'Well, of course I realise that he's never serious, but it's no wonder that he turns so many heads, for he's quite the beau ideal! We've seen him here once or twice visiting his grandmother, Lady Carteret, at Rushdene Park, though not very lately. I dare say Lady Carteret will call, by the way, once word gets to her that you are staying with me.'

Lydia did not look overwhelmed with joy at this prospect, and her face fell still further when the Middleham children were brought into the room by their nurse for a few moments. They were attractive children, a girl of three years old with dark curls and an elfin face, and a boy scarcely two, who was as fair as his sister was dark. After a momentary show of shyness, little Marianne prattled away quite happily to Alethea, who was used to children and generally knew how to interest them; but Robin flung his arms round his nurse's knees, burying his face in her apron and refusing to look up even for his father.

'Come, that's scarcely a civil greeting for your Aunt,' said Sir Roger in a coaxing tone.

'Oh, don't mind me,' said Lydia. 'I'm not at all upset if they don't choose to notice me. You must know that I'm no use with children — I fear they bore me extremely.'

This could scarcely be thought of as a tactful speech, and for a moment Eleanor Middleham looked hurt. But she was too used to her sister's ways to take serious offence, so she kissed the little ones and sent them off to the nursery again.

'What a delightful pair,' said Alethea, with some idea of pouring oil on troubled waters, although her admiration was quite sincere. 'I think little Marianne favours you, Eleanor.'

This happy remark succeeded in banishing any ill will aroused by Lydia's gaucherie, and soon the two sisters were talking away again at a great rate, while Sir Roger pursued a more leisurely conversation with Alethea.

'Do you ride, Cousin Alethea?' he asked presently.

She nodded. 'Why, yes. I live in the country, you know, and there one must either ride or be prepared to walk very long distances.'

He looked pleased. 'Then you will perhaps like to ride my wife's mare while you are here — the poor beast hasn't had nearly enough exercise of late. She is very gentle, I promise you, an ideal mount for a lady.'

'You are most kind — yes, I should like that. But what about my cousin Lydia?'

'Oh, Lydia doesn't care for horse riding. But I'm sure she and Eleanor will have plenty to occupy them, should you wish to slip away any time for an hour or so. Only listen to them now!'

The rest of the day passed away pleasantly. Sir Roger accompanied the two girls on a stroll in the grounds during the afternoon while his wife took her customary rest; afterwards they sat down to a quiet family dinner followed by cards and conversation. It was one of the most relaxed evenings that Alethea had spent since leaving her own home, and she felt all the benefit of it. She told herself that a few such peaceful, uneventful days would be a tonic after the hurly burly of London life; little did she know how soon that peace was to be shattered.

Events were set in train the next morning, when the ladies were sitting in a parlour at the front of the house. Hearing the sound of horses and wheels approaching along the drive, Lydia and Eleanor hastened to the window. A carriage with crested panels was approaching at a sedate pace, closely attended by two gentlemen on horseback.

'Why, it's Lady Carteret's carriage!' exclaimed Eleanor. 'I told you she would be here, Lydia, when she knew of your arrival, but I never dreamt it would be quite so soon!'

But Lydia had made a surprising and welcome discovery of her own. 'Lud, who do you think it is with her? Devenish — and Vivyan, of all people! What in the world can he be doing here?'

She ran to the nearest mirror and began patting her hair into place. Alethea felt a pang of dismay. There would be trouble if her Aunt found out about this, and had not Lydia said that her sister Eleanor was a tale-bearer?

In a moment the visitors were among them, and a footman was despatched to summon Sir Roger, who was with his secretary in the library. Lady Carteret, a tall, dignified woman in her early seventies with a lively eye and a smile that suggested a resemblance to her grandson, was all affability. She had come over, it seemed, with the intention of engaging them all to dine with her that same evening.

'Such a fortunate chance,' she remarked, with a twinkle in her eye, 'that James should have chosen this very time to pay me one of his all too infrequent visits. And to have brought with him Mr Allerton, too, whose family has, I know, such a long-standing friendship with your own. We shall make a most agreeable party — that is, my dear Lady Middleham, if you should feel equal to a coach ride of ten minutes or so.'

Eleanor insisted that the exertion would be nothing compared to the benefit she would derive from an evening away from home, and so it was settled. Sir Roger, who had been talking of horse flesh to Devenish and Allerton, now offered to show them the latest additions to his stable. They accepted, and were about to follow him from the room when he turned to Alethea.

'Would you perhaps care to accompany us, Cousin Alethea? I can show you the mare I was speaking of earlier.'

Alethea glanced at her hostess, who nodded. 'Yes, by all means go — you, too, Lydia, if you wish, then Lady Carteret and I can have a quiet little coze together.'

Lydia rose with alacrity to accompany the others. 'Not that I'm the least little bit interested in horses,' she whispered to Alethea as they made their way to the side entrance of the house, 'but since Vivyan's come all this way just to see me, I may as well give him the opportunity of snatching a word or two, away from Eleanor's ears.'

It was an opportunity that Allerton soon took once they were walking along the path which led to the stables, since here there was not sufficient room to walk five abreast. He and Lydia fell back a few paces, leaving the others to go on ahead.

'Do I collect that Sir Roger is about to sell you a mare?' asked Devenish of Alethea, with a quizzical look.

'Sell? Good God, no!' Sir Roger laughed, 'It's m'wife's mare, but naturally the beast lacks exercise at present, and Miss Newnham has kindly promised to take it out now and then during the few days she's to be with us.'

'So you number horseriding among your talents, ma'am?'

'I learned to ride from necessity, sir, and in the beginning I failed lamentably to exhibit any kind of talent for it,' answered Alethea, with a laugh. 'Had it not been for the perseverance of my brothers, I fear I should never have succeeded.'

'Your brothers — ah, yes,' murmured Devenish. 'You have spoken of them before. I think you said you have no sisters, Miss Newnham?'

Alethea shook her head. 'I've often wished I had.'

'Can't think why,' put in Sir Roger, with a chuckle. 'Far as I can see, sisters are for ever squabbling with each other. What say you, Devenish?'

'I fear I'm scarcely qualified to speak, as I don't possess any sisters.'

'No, but you've had ample opportunity to study other people's,' began Sir Roger; then, realising that this was a somewhat equivocal remark, he coughed and hastily changed the subject. 'Staying long with Lady Carteret this time?'

Devenish looked amused. 'A day or two — my plans are uncertain.'

They had reached the stables by this time, and the head groom came out to speak to Sir Roger, leaving Alethea and Devenish standing together a little to one side.

'There are several tolerably pretty villages within a very few miles of here, Miss Newnham. If you are to see the best of the surrounding country on your rides, you will require a guide who knows the district well.'

'Oh, yes. But I'm quite sure I shall have one in Sir Roger.'

'Of course,' agreed Devenish, smoothly. 'But Middleham's a busy fellow, bowed down by domestic responsibilities. Should he find himself obliged to abandon you to the tender mercies of a groom, I would be most happy to take his place.'

'You are very good, Sir James,' she said, guardedly.

He bowed. 'Not at all. My dear young lady, am I not pledged to give you a better understanding of me?'

'It's a pledge *I* did not require.' She answered him primly enough, but her eyes sparkled with amusement. He really was the most absurd creature, even though she was quite determined not to allow him to flirt with her as he did with so many others.

'Alas, no. I can make no headway at all with you. I can only say with Orsino "Still so cruel?"'

She completed the quotation. '"Still so constant, lord."'

He smiled lazily. 'Ah, yes, you would know your *Twelfth Night*. Tell me, ma'am, do you suppose Olivia really did mean to spurn Orsino, or was she simply employing an age-old feminine technique for drawing the poor fellow deeper into her net?'

Alethea laughed, then pondered for a moment. 'No, I don't think so,' she said, at last. 'As far as I recollect, there was nothing either in her character or her later actions to suggest it. But are you serious, sir? I take leave to doubt it! If you are, what evidence would you bring forward to support your view?'

'Evidence — ah, yes. You wouldn't allow me to offer as evidence my own knowledge of the female sex, I suppose?' His hazel eyes held a twinkle as they met hers for a second. 'No, I see you would not, and I can't altogether blame you. You would require textual evidence, of course. Well, to go further with this discussion, we need to consider the text of the play together. Perhaps we may have an opportunity to do so this evening, since you are all to dine with my grandmother.'

Alethea shook her head. 'I doubt if the rest of the party would think that very civil of us.'

'Ah, I see what it is, ma'am. You don't wish to pursue the discussion further, thinking that I may prove my point.'

'It's no such thing — how dare you! You really are the most teasing person!'

'Acquit me,' he said, with mock solemnity. 'I haven't the temerity to tease one of your disposition.'

'Oh?' She abandoned for the moment her attempt to adopt a repressive attitude towards him. 'I take leave to doubt that, sir! Pray, what do you make of my disposition?'

'I think that must wait until another time,' he said in an undertone as Sir Roger, having finished his conversation with the groom, turned towards them again.

A stable lad was leading out Eleanor's mare, and Sir Roger invited Alethea's opinion of the animal.

'She's a pet, isn't she?' replied Alethea, stroking the mare's nose. 'I can see that she's as every bit as gentle as you claim. What did you say her name is, Cousin Roger?'

'Dulcetta. But let me see you try her, Cousin. Just a turn or two about the yard.'

'Well, I'm not really dressed for it, but that's no great matter. Very well, then, for I'd like to see how we suit, Dulcetta and I.'

The mare was made ready and Sir Roger assisted Alethea to mount. They all watched as she took the animal quietly round the stableyard without the slightest difficulty.

'Capital!' he said, after having watched her for a few minutes. 'You have an excellent seat, and I shall certainly have no qualms for your safety. What do you say if we go out for a ride later on, when my wife's taking her afternoon rest?'

'Oh, I should like it of all things!' exclaimed Alethea, as she dismounted. 'But what would Lydia find to amuse her,' she added, as an afterthought, 'if her sister's resting?'

'I dare say she'll not mind for once, eh, Lydia? Lydia, I say!'

He had to repeat her name, because she and Allerton were still so engrossed in each other that they seemed oblivious of everything else. She looked up at last with a vague smile, asking what he wanted. He explained, and she shook her head.

'Oh, there's no need to mind me,' she said, with unwonted generosity. 'Most likely I shall find some shady nook in the garden and be quite content to pass the afternoon there.'

The faintest of frowns creased Devenish's usually inscrutable brow.

'But why don't we all go?' demanded Allerton, coming to life again. 'We could go in my curricle, Lydia, since you don't care for riding — that is, if you can face the thought of jolting over country lanes.'

He looked at her doubtfully for a moment, but to his delight she nodded.

'I think so — after all, I suppose we shouldn't cover any great distance.'

'Certainly not, for your cousin will be strange to her mount,' Sir Roger reminded her.

'Oh, as to that,' put in Alethea, 'with such an amenable creature as Dulcetta there can be no trouble.'

She gave the mare a final pat before it was led away.

'Well, no, so I think. But should you find any difficulty, there will be two of us to keep an eye on you — I take it you'll ride with us, Devenish?'

Devenish replied with alacrity that nothing would give him greater pleasure, and a time was fixed there and then for the two gentlemen to present themselves at the house.

'And now I'd like to show you my new bay,' said Sir Roger. 'It may be dull work for you two girls, so I shan't take it amiss if you want to stroll back to the house and join the ladies.'

'Oh, be sure we know when we're not wanted, don't we, Alethea?' said Lydia, with a saucy toss of her dark curls.

'No, I say!' protested Allerton. 'No such thing!'

She had linked her arm in Alethea's and was turning away, but she paused to flash an enchanting smile in his direction. Sir Roger looked after her thoughtfully for a moment.

Chapter XVI

Alethea was enjoying herself. The afternoon was warm, but not too hot, the lanes leafy and fragrant with May blossom. Her mount gave her no trouble; in fact, she was a sufficiently good horsewoman to have managed a much more lively animal than the gentle Dulcetta.

She found herself enjoying her company, too. The curricle went ahead of the riders on the road; occasionally either Sir Roger or Devenish would ride alongside it for a while before dropping back to join the other two.

During his intervals at her side, Sir Roger kept up an interesting commentary on the scenes through which they were passing. Devenish's conversation was, as usual, entertaining, but on a less trivial note than formerly. He began by asking her if she had read any of Paul Tracy's poetry.

'Why, yes,' she replied, surprised. 'I've been reading some very lately — Mr Tracy was good enough to give me one of his books.'

'Indeed.' His characteristic drawl was very much in evidence. 'And may I ask what is your opinion of his work?'

Alethea hesitated. 'I'm not really qualified to pass an opinion on a subject of which I know so little.'

He laughed, and she thought how much more attractive he looked when his expression was animated. 'I say fustian to that, ma'am! The opinion of a serious reader must always be worthy of attention, at least. Come, now.'

She realised that this was very much what she had said to young Simon Allerton not so long ago.

'Very well. I thought Mr Tracy's poems showed both originality and power. I was somewhat surprised at the — the vigour of some of them,' she added.

'Yes, it is unexpected,' he agreed. 'But writers themselves are often quite different in character from what their works would lead one to imagine.'

'Oh, so you have read the poems yourself?' asked Alethea, incredulously.

'Why not? You were not supposing me to be totally illiterate, ma'am?'

'How absurd you are at times! No, not that, of course! But I hardly imagined that —' she stopped, afraid of giving offence, and glanced at him to see how he was taking this.

His expression showed nothing but amusement.

'You think me a frippery fellow who never gives a thought to anything more serious than the set of a coat or the points of a horse,' he accused her. 'Come, now, you may as well confess it! I see it writ plainly enough in your face — and that,' he added, with a warmth in his eyes which disconcerted her, 'is the only plain thing I do see there, for the rest is perfection.'

This outrageous flattery had the effect of forcing the truth from Alethea. 'Yes, I did think so,' she admitted, defiantly. 'After all, everyone calls you Beau Devenish, and that title indicates a pre-occupation with fashion.'

'A touching tribute,' he replied, mockingly. 'Do you know anything about icebergs, Miss Newnham?'

'*Icebergs?*'

She was so amazed by this non sequitur that her hold on the rein momentarily slackened and Dulcetta, docile as she was, swerved slightly. Quickly Devenish put out his hand to right matters, and for a moment it rested on hers. He removed it almost at once, as she was soon in control again, of the horse, if not of her emotions, for that brief touch had stirred something within her. She fought it back angrily.

'Icebergs?' she repeated, in acid tones.

He nodded. 'I don't claim to be an expert on the subject myself. But I've always understood that only the very tip of an iceberg appears on the surface.'

'And you mean to draw a parallel with yourself, I collect?' She sounded scornful.

'I certainly intended that, but if the present climate continues, my figure of speech is like to become a reality,' he answered, with a doleful expression. 'I don't know how it is, ma'am, but I seem to have the unfortunate gift of putting you quite out of humour with my poor self. And yet "my true intent is all for your delight", as another poet said.'

She had to laugh at that; and just then Sir Roger, who had been riding ahead with the curricle, dropped back again to join them. Devenish, who knew to a nicety when to let well alone in his dealings with the fair sex, rode forward to take his place, leaving Alethea to think over what had passed between them.

She was puzzled. He was trying to flirt with her, of course; that much was clear. And presumably since pretty speeches did not appear to serve his purpose, he was searching for another means to interest her, an approach through her intellect. But why go to so much trouble? There were plenty of other females, as she had been informed, who were only too eager to engage with him in this kind of light dalliance. Why expend time and effort on a girl who was determined not to respond to his overtures? That it must involve considerable effort for him she was certain, for she did indeed consider him a frippery fellow, as he had phrased it. Fashion, the pleasures of the Town and the pursuit of young women were obviously the chief preoccupations of his life. To pretend to any intellectual interests was the merest sham, and she wondered indignantly that he could hope to take her in by such a pitiful ruse. She would show him, though, that she saw through him, and had not the least intention of allowing herself to be known as Devenish's latest flirt.

She did her best to put these wise precepts into practice when they met again that same evening at Rushdene Park. Although she found herself seated next to Devenish at the dining table, she contrived to avoid a tête-à-tête, either by joining in the general conversation or, whenever this lapsed for a few moments, by giving all her attention to her other neighbour, Sir Roger.

In this way, they had reached the third course without more than the barest civilities passing between them. Then he leaned towards her.

'I trust you're fond of strawberries, Miss Newnham.'

She gave a little start, for at that moment she had been studying Lydia and Allerton, who still seemed to be so absorbed in each other that they scarcely noticed the rest of the party.

'Strawberries? Oh, yes, I like them prodigiously.'

'Good, for that is to be our next course, and I particularly wish it to put you in a good humour,' he said, in a low voice.

She raised her brows. 'I am not out of humour, sir. Why should you suppose so?'

'No? Well, perhaps you're not in general; but I can quite see that you mean to ignore me. I wish you will tell me what I have done to get in your bad books.'

'Now you are talking nonsense again,' she replied, in a matter of fact way.

'Ah, yes, and you don't like nonsense. We established that long since, did we not? I must think of something Johnsonian to say, or perhaps scribble a verse or two in the manner of Paul Tracy before I can command your attention.'

She was amused, but could not resist trying to give him a set-down. 'Pray don't put yourself to the trouble of such a Herculean task on my account, Sir James.'

'Ah, now you're showing your claws, ma'am! But you underrate me, you know. I have written verse in my time, even if it was very bad verse, as my tutor at Oxford did not scruple to inform me.'

'So you were at Oxford?'

He nodded. 'They were unable to think of any way to avoid having me, although much midnight oil was burnt in considering the matter.'

This time she could not help laughing.

'That's better,' he approved. 'You have the most enchanting way of laughing, Miss Newnham. Your nose wrinkles and your eyes dance — such fine grey eyes, too. But —' he added, as her expression hardened at this unwanted compliment — 'I am sorry to say that they can look distressingly stony at times.'

She turned away, ignoring him for the rest of the meal. When it was over, the ladies retired to the drawing-room, leaving the men to sit over the wine. On this occasion, they were not absent for very long; when they came into the drawing-room, Devenish was seen to be carrying a book under his arm.

'Are you about to read to us, Sir James?' asked Eleanor, who was comfortably seated in an ample wing chair with her legs supported on a footstool.

'God forbid!' exclaimed Allerton fervently.

'No, ma'am, I had no intention of inflicting so much tedium on you,' replied Devenish, seating himself on the sofa between Lydia and Alethea. 'I merely brought in this volume of

Shakespeare's play *Twelfth Night* in order to continue a discussion I was having with Miss Newnham.'

'Lud, a discussion on Shakespeare!' said Lydia, in mock dismay. 'Pray let me sit somewhere else where I may not disturb you.'

She moved to a chair close to Eleanor, and Allerton drew one up beside her. Soon the rest of the party were chatting together, leaving Alethea and Devenish to themselves.

This both embarrassed and annoyed Alethea. She certainly did not wish to be singled out by Devenish in so marked a way. Surely she had made it abundantly clear to him already that she had no intention of taking part in one of his meaningless flirtations? He must find someone else for that game; it was not to her taste.

At first, therefore, he found her disinclined to say much; but he pursued his nonsensical thesis with so much wit and real knowledge of the play that before long she could not help relaxing her guard and entering into the spirit of the discussion. It ended by his closing the book on a mutual agreement to differ.

'At any rate,' he said, 'we have both learnt something, if not about Olivia's character, then at least about each other's.'

'Yes,' she agreed, laughing. 'I have learnt that nothing you say, sir, may be taken seriously!'

'No, no, that is too severe.'

She shook her head. 'Not a whit! And what, pray, have you learnt about me? That I am obstinate, for instance?'

'Possibly.' His eyes, unusually serious, met hers and held them for a moment. 'But everything I do learn about you, ma'am, only serves to convince me that I would like to know more. Will you not give me the opportunity?'

To her consternation, once again Alethea felt that faint stirring of the senses. She made no reply, but hastily looked away from him towards the others. Eleanor unconsciously came to her aid at that moment by asking if their literary discussion was at an end. Devenish assented briefly, rising to place the volume on an occasional table. He seemed a trifle subdued, thought Alethea; or perhaps it was just that her own sensitivity was abnormally heightened for the moment.

Lady Carteret suggested that they should have some music, and Lydia was eventually persuaded to sit down at the pianoforte. Allerton came to stand beside her, ostensibly to turn over the pages; but in fact he frequently neglected this duty because he could not take his eyes off the performer.

'Delightful, my dear,' said Lady Carteret, when Lydia had finished, 'Will you not oblige us now, Miss Newnham?'

A quick panic rose in Alethea. If she sat down to play, she was quite sure that the irrepressible Devenish would be standing close beside her with the same excuse as Allerton had used while Lydia was performing. It was not to be risked in her present mood, so she refused as vigorously as civility would allow.

Once again, Eleanor inadvertently came to her rescue by suggesting that the three gentlemen should join in singing some catches and glees.

'I so much enjoy male voices, do not you?' she asked her hostess. 'And perhaps Alethea would not object to playing the accompaniment.'

The men demurred a little, but finally agreed, and Alethea felt bound to do the same. Since they chose catches which were well known to them all, they were not obliged to peer over her shoulder at the music, and she began gradually to recover her poise.

'Encore!' cried Eleanor, when they had ended and made their bow with a flourish. 'I had no notion, Sir James, that you had such a fine voice! Will you not sing something for us on your own?'

Devenish hastily disclaimed the compliment, saying that he had no wish to inflict any further suffering on the company; but Lady Carteret, pleased, like most grandmothers, at any tribute to a member of the junior branch of her family, persuaded him to give them just one song.

'It must be short then, ma'am,' he conceded, going to the pianoforte and sorting through some music, 'since I know that some, at least, of our recent performers must be suffering from dry throats, and will require a remedy.'

He selected a sheet from among the music, and handed it to Alethea with a bow.

'May I hope to prevail on you to accompany me, Miss Newnham?'

She accepted it hesitantly, scanning the sheet.

'Oh, dear. I'm not at all sure that I can manage this — I don't know it —'

'Shall I leave you for a few minutes to try it over to yourself?' he asked, encouragingly. 'I'm quite sure you'll manage famously.'

She placed the music on the stand and obediently sat down to make an attempt at playing it. At first she found some difficulty in concentrating; but this was made easier in a few seconds, as he walked away to order some wine for his male guests. By the time he returned to her side, she had mastered the piece and was ready to accompany him.

'Appropriate, is it not?' he asked her, as she poised her fingers over the keys.

She nodded. He had chosen *Oh, Mistress Mine*, the clown's song from *Twelfth Night*.

She had to agree with Eleanor that he certainly possessed a very good voice. There was a certain mocking quality in it, too, that fitted both the words of the song and the personality of the singer. Her enjoyment of the performance was marred, though, by a guilty consciousness that he was deliberately aiming the song's message at her.

'What is love? 'tis not hereafter;

Present mirth hath present laughter;

What's to come is still unsure.

In delay there lies no plenty;

Then come kiss me, sweet and twenty,

Youth's a stuff will not endure –

Not endure.'

There was no doubt about it, she thought uneasily in the privacy of her bedchamber that night, she had underestimated his power to charm. He was a dangerous man — very — and she had best keep out of his way in future.

Chapter XVII

Her misgivings faded in the optimistic light of a new day, and her thoughts were given a new direction when they all set out soon after breakfast to call on one or two of the Middleham's nearest neighbours. They were all pleasant, friendly people, and there was no lack of invitations to dine or attend evening parties. Owing to the shortness of the young ladies' visit, these had to be regretfully declined; but Eleanor had come prepared with one of her own for the following evening. Fortunately there were no previous engagements to prevent acceptance, so that by the time they left the last house they were able to expect the company of at least a dozen friends of varying ages on Saturday.

'As long as you're sure you won't find it too fatiguing, my love,' remarked Sir Roger, handing his wife solicitously into the coach.

'Oh, gracious, no, Roger! The only thing I find infinitely fatiguing is the boredom of my own company. I am so glad you girls could come,' she added, turning to her sister and Alethea. 'I haven't been so diverted in months, I assure you! I only wish you could stay longer — but, there, I mustn't be greedy, and Mama did explain.'

They reached home to find two callers on their own doorstep. Devenish and Allerton had ridden over so that Allerton could take his leave of the Middlehams since he was to return to Town that afternoon.

'Oh, dear, and do you go, too, Sir James?' asked Eleanor, when they were all sitting in the parlour. 'What a melancholy business these partings are, to be sure!'

'No, ma'am, I am settled here for another day or two,' replied Devenish. 'My grandmother refused to part with me just yet, although I'm sure she must find a man about the house more of a penance than a pleasure.'

'That's all you know of it,' laughed Eleanor. 'Why she's for ever talking of you, and wishing she could see you more often. There's nothing solitary females like more than to have a man about the house. But since you're to stay, may we prevail on you and Lady Carteret to join us here for an evening party tomorrow? Nothing formal, you understand, just a group of neighbours — the Lesleys, the Mainwarings and the Colefords — all amiable people, and known well to your grandmother, if not to yourself.'

Devenish accepted gracefully on his own account, and promised to let them know later if Lady Carteret would also be at liberty to come.

They stayed almost an hour chatting together, without any opportunity for private conversation between Lydia and Vivyan Allerton, although his eyes never left her face; and for her part she seemed much quieter than usual. As for Alethea, she never looked once at Devenish, yet to her annoyance she was all the time conscious of his presence in the room.

At length they rose to go. Vivyan took leave of Lydia last of all, holding her hand much longer than mere courtesy required as he bowed over it.

'We shall meet again in Town,' he said in the voice of one who would be held in suspended animation until then.

'Oh, yes. You will be at Alethea's ball on Thursday, won't you? I hope your sisters enjoy the Masquerade this evening — I do wish I had been coming!'

'So do I,' he replied, in a low voice. 'It will be stupid and boring without you.'

He released her hand at last, and with many backward glances managed to take himself off. They all watched from the window as he and Devenish rode down the drive.

Eleanor then retired for her afternoon rest, and Sir Roger went out on some estate business, leaving the two girls together. Lydia began prowling restlessly round the room, a sullen scowl marring her pretty face.

'It is beyond anything tedious in the country!' she exclaimed, pettishly. 'I knew it would be.'

'You seem to have been tolerably well entertained up to now,' answered Alethea, soothingly. 'And there's to be a party tomorrow evening, with plenty of new faces.'

'Country parties!' scoffed her cousin. ''Pon 'rep, I am amazed that Devenish, of all people, should consent to attend one! As for his singing yesterday evening, it's the most remarkable thing I ever did see — only wait until I tell everybody in Town! They will never believe me!'

'What should be so remarkable about that? It is quite customary for gentlemen to sing at evening parties, among friends.'

'Yes, but *Devenish*! I ask you! It is not at all in his line.'

'I should suppose,' said Alethea, severely, 'that it is in *any* gentleman's line to accede to a request of that kind made by a lady who's a visitor to his house. And your sister Eleanor did press him, as I'm sure you'll own.'

'Yes, yes, Alethea, but you don't know Devenish as I do! He has not the slightest regard for what is commonly done, and will edge himself out of such tiresome obligations in the most accomplished way, without ever giving offence. If he does anything to oblige anyone else, it is usually because he has some motive of his own.'

'What an odious character you give him!'

'Yes, well he *is* odious, really. Oh, of course he's the most prodigious charmer, and all that kind of thing, and has turned more heads than there are bonnets to fit them. But he's utterly selfish and — and unscrupulous!'

Alethea made no reply to this. It was very much what she had been telling herself during the past few days; strange that it should in some way hurt her to hear it from someone else.

'He's doing his best now to get up a flirtation with you,' went on Lydia, disagreeably. 'You can see he doesn't care who it is.'

'Thank you. A very graceful compliment, if I may say so, Cousin. Did you study for it, or did it come by the fair light of nature?'

'I must say you know how to give one a sarcastic set-down yourself, Alethea! But I didn't really mean to be disparaging towards you — it was just a manner of speaking. What I meant was that one would think he'd leave you alone, as you're not at all in his style. Though why in the world,' she added, wonderingly, 'you don't amuse yourself by indulging in a little harmless flirtation with him for a while, is more than I can understand. What possible harm can there be, so long as you don't allow yourself to become too deeply involved? And I dare swear you're by far too level headed for that, in spite of your romantical notions.'

Alethea sighed. 'We've had this conversation before, Lydia. I wish you will understand that I haven't the faintest desire to have a flirtation with any man, least of all with Beau Devenish.' She invested the name with scorn. 'To my mind, flirtations are stupid indulgences of vanity at best, and at worst they are a contemptible travesty of feelings which should be deep and sincere. By what right does any man so misuse his manhood — or woman her womanhood, for that matter — as to entrap some unwary member of the opposite sex with false protestations and hypocritical attentions? I tell you I will have no part in so despicable an artifice!'

Lydia looked at her in astonishment for a moment. 'Here's a pother,' she said, with a shrug. 'I can't help feeling, you know, that some of what you said was to my address.'

'If the cap fits,' retorted Alethea, still feeling angry.

'Well, perhaps it may,' said Lydia, in a miserable tone. 'I have been encouraging Vivyan, I'll grant you that. But —'

She paused for a few moments, while Alethea said nothing, waiting for her to continue.

'Oh, how I wish I could have gone with him to this Masquerade!' exclaimed Lydia at last, striding up and down the room in frustration. 'Do you know, I almost decided to creep away and hire a chaise to take me back to Town so that I could go, after all? When I came here, I certainly had some such scheme in mind, for I was as mad as fire with Mama and determined to disobey her, by hook or by crook.'

'I'm glad you didn't — it would have caused an upheaval! But what made you change your mind, may I ask?'

'Oh, I don't know.' Lydia shrugged again. 'It would have been so tiresome to arrange, for one thing. There was the chaise to be hired secretly, and then I would have needed to take a maid, and she might have blurted out the plan; and then I would have had to take you into my confidence to concoct some tale for Eleanor, and then my brother-in-law might have found out, and that would have meant no end of a fuss. No!' she finished, explosively, 'I just couldn't face the endless tedium of arranging it all — nothing in the world can be worth so much effort! Only I don't see why Mama should have everything her own way, and the sooner I am married and quit of her interference, the better!'

'You will have a husband's interference then,' Alethea reminded her.

'Oh, I could manage a husband,' said Lydia, confidently.

'I wonder? They are not near so obliging as suitors,' laughed Alethea. '"Men are April when they woo, December when they wed", as Shakespeare tells us.'

'Poetry again! I tell you what it is, Alethea — you've a deal of knowledge conned from books, but you'll find it won't help you when it comes to dealing with situations in real life,' said Lydia, scathingly.

Alethea sobered. 'You may be right. But why don't we take a stroll in the park, Lydia? The exercise will help to draw off some of your spleen.'

'No, I don't feel like walking, and, anyway, it's too odiously hot today. You go, if you want to. I'd rather be on my own, at present — I'm in no mood for company, and shall only quarrel with you.'

Alethea went, not sorry to be quit of her cousin in this present mood. There would be little pleasure in a solitary walk, so she decided to go for a ride instead. As she made her way to the stables, she noticed how oppressive the atmosphere had become and almost turned back to sit indoors; but the thought of having to put up with Lydia's sulks was too much for her.

'Shouldn't be surprised, Miss, if we don't get a storm coming up afore long,' said Perkins as he saddled the mare. 'Was ye thinking of going far?'

'Oh, no, only a few miles or so along the lanes,' she answered. 'I shan't need a groom.'

Perkins raised his bushy eyebrows at this, but he was too well trained to question it. Miss was used to riding, as anyone could see who had watched her on horseback; and being a country bred young lady, no doubt, she was accustomed to riding out alone when she was going only short distances. So he stared after her as Dulcetta clattered merrily away over the cobbles of the yard and down the drive, thinking how trim and pretty the mare's rider looked and what a pleasant young lady she was.

The drive was lined with chestnut trees which sheltered Alethea from the fierceness of the sun's rays until she reached the gates which led into the lane. Here the heat seemed to strike her with the force of a blow. She hesitated for a moment, thinking that her cousin had been right in saying the afternoon was too hot for exercise out of doors. Perhaps she ought to go back. But apart from the unattractive prospect of returning to Lydia's company, her conscience would prick her for putting Perkins to the trouble of saddling the mare all for nothing. She shrugged, and turned into the lane.

She had gone only a short distance along it, though in some discomfort from the heat, when she saw that not far ahead lay a wood stretching beside the road. She decided to make this her objective; the mere sight of its green branches made her feel cooler already.

When she reached the wood and turned thankfully into its shade, however, she found that even here the air was still heavy and oppressive. Not so much as the ghost of a breeze disturbed the foliage. There really was no bearing this sultry atmosphere; she would ride just a little way into the wood, and then return home. Perhaps already Lydia had recovered her temper. If not, they must try to keep out of each other's way.

Her thoughts strayed from Lydia to the events of the past two days, showing a regrettable tendency to dwell on Beau Devenish. Every conversation they had shared was reviewed and subjected to a searching scrutiny. Looking for what? Alethea asked herself sharply, and from then on she made a determined effort to shut him out. Surprisingly, this seemed even more exhausting than her former preoccupation with the subject. Every new train of thought seemed to lead back to him in the end. She felt out of all patience with herself.

A distant rumble of thunder recalled her sharply to her surroundings. She reined in Dulcetta and turned to look back in the direction of the lane she had left. There was no sign of it; she seemed to be deep in the wood. She looked anxiously about her, then saw that the path she was now following was much narrower than the one by which she had entered the wood. In her abstraction, she must have strayed from the bridle path on to a side track — indeed she might have followed several. She had no notion which way she had turned, or what direction to take now in order to reach the lane.

She was lost.

Chapter VIII

For a while she circled about looking for the bridle path; or, if not that, for a wider track than the one she was at present following, one which would appear well used enough to indicate that it led out of the wood. When this proved unavailing, she halted the mare, considering what to do.

A wood was certainly not the best place to choose for being caught in a thunderstorm. She must get out of it as soon as possible. But would she manage this more quickly by continuing along her present path, or by making some attempt to retrace her route she had taken? Going back would not be easy, for she had no idea how much she might have changed direction in reaching this point. Her thoughts had been elsewhere. To continue on the present track, though, might only carry her still deeper into the wood. To her anxious gaze, it looked equally dense on either side.

She must make some decision, she told herself; and so she applied her own particular maxim that it was always preferable to go forward rather than back. Urging the lethargic Dulcetta to a smarter pace, she continued on the path she had been following.

By now, the sky had become overcast with thunder clouds, plunging the wood into stygian gloom. Alethea felt an oppression of spirits that matched the atmosphere. In spite of her country upbringing, she had never liked thunderstorms; they unnerved her, and to be lost in a wood, alone, while a storm was brewing had for her a nightmare quality. She had more than her share of commonsense, but underneath her control she could feel the faint stirrings of panic. It was not an agreeable sensation.

Low rumblings of thunder continued, though still in the distance, while she guided Dulcetta along the path and peered anxiously through the gathering gloom for any sign of a wider track. Presently she came to a narrow path going off at right angles to the one she was following. She checked for a moment, undecided which to take. Never change horses in mid-stream, she reminded herself; smiling wanly at the absurdity of trying to follow any advice offered by proverbs, as all too often it was conflicting. Nevertheless, she did keep to her present path.

The thunder was creeping nearer now, like an imprisoned giant shaking off its shackles. A thin flicker of distant lightning momentarily relieved the gloom of the wood. Alethea shivered, urging Dulcetta to a canter. The horse responded, laying back its ears; it, too, seemed to be affected by the approaching storm, for once or twice it quivered. Every time this happened, Alethea felt her panic rising. She gritted her teeth and fought it down.

After a short distance, the track bent round in another direction; and there before her at last lay the bridle path which she had so far sought in vain. Her spirit lifted. She had only to follow this, and it must lead her out of the wood.

Then they sank again as she realised that there was no way of knowing in which direction to follow it. To right or to left? A closer rumble of thunder made her decide hastily, and she turned right. She set Dulcetta at the gallop, hoping fervently that the ground would be even enough to safeguard the animal from a stumble. Her one compelling thought now was to get out of the wood before the storm was upon her in full force.

It seemed unlikely that she would manage to do this, for the trees showed no sign of thinning; while the thunder rolled even nearer, accompanied by periodic flashes of sheet lightning. Panic threatened her once more.

She was so occupied in grappling with it that at first she failed to hear the soft thud of hoofbeats approaching from somewhere on her right. When the sound at length did penetrate her consciousness, it brought with it added fears. Who could be abroad in this gloomy, deserted wood in such wild weather? It might be a highwayman, or some cutthroat felon.

A horse and rider suddenly loomed up before her on the path. A thin scream, which she tried too late to stifle, left her lips. Her trembling hands tugged at Dulcetta's rein, causing the frightened mare to rear so that its rider was almost thrown.

In what seemed one movement, the other rider flung himself from his horse and rushed to her side, gripping her firmly about the waist with his left arm while he forced Dulcetta's head down with his right. Seeing that Alethea, though scared, was still firmly in the saddle, he released her and gave his attention to quietening the horse. It was only then that Alethea had time to realise that the rider whom she had thought so sinister was in fact Beau Devenish.

Under his firm, confident hand the mare soon settled. He gave the reins back to Alethea, staring at her with a deep frown on his brow.

'What in God's name are you doing here alone, Miss Newnham? Is something amiss at Roxeth Place? Lady Middleham — she is perhaps —?'

He let the question trail away as she shook her head. She could not answer him for the moment; she was still too shaken. A long tumbril sound of thunder rolled about them, followed by the most vivid flash of lightning yet. She started violently, and he put his hand on the rein again.

'No, n-nothing's wrong at the house.' She choked back a sob. 'I came out for a r-ride, and lost my way in this wood —'

He nodded, wasting no further time in explanations. 'Do you think you can manage the mare a bit longer, ma'am? The wood adjoins my grandmother's grounds — no distance now, if you can hold on.'

She nodded, keeping a firm grip on herself.

'Yes — yes, I'll be all right now. You — you startled me, and the storm —'

He swung himself back into the saddle and wheeled the horse to ride alongside Dulcetta.

'We'll take it fast,' he said, in a voice very unlike his usual drawl. 'The rain's not far off, and I haven't so much as a cloak to protect you.'

She was still shaken by her experiences and her fear of the storm, but everything seemed better now that he was beside her. They followed the track for a short distance and suddenly came to the edge of the wood and a high wall with a gate set in it. As he dismounted to open the gate and let her through a streak of lightning forked down the sky. Alethea jumped violently, and once again Devenish had to steady Dulcetta.

'Not much farther now,' he said, in an encouraging tone. 'That drive leads up to the stables — we may just reach there in time.'

He closed the gate, remounted his horse, and galloped beside Alethea up the drive, one hand on Dulcetta's rein.

As they reached the entrance to the stables, a clap of thunder like the crack of doom sounded above their heads. It was as though it had opened the skies; rain poured down relentlessly, hitting the cobbles of the yard and bouncing back.

Devenish emitted a loud whistle, and several grooms came running. One, brighter than the others, ran back into the harness room and returned with two large capes. Devenish, dismounted hurriedly, seized one of these and flung it over Alethea before lifting her bodily from the saddle. As he did so, the groom set the other cape about his master's shoulders, but Devenish dragged most of it round Alethea as he ran with her into the harness room.

A couple of grooms who were working there moved unobtrusively away to another part of the stable, so that Devenish and Alethea had the place to themselves. He guided her to a bench against the wall and removed the cape which he had flung over her head and shoulders.

'Are you very wet?' he asked. 'I fear your bonnet is ruined.'

She ran shaking hands over the sleeves and bodice of her gown. They were soaked through.

'Yes, I — I am, but it d-doesn't signify. My b-bonnet — I don't care about that either —'

She broke off with a gasp, as another violent flash of lightning lit up the interior of the harness room with a ghastly light. Devenish seized a horse cloth and suspended it before the window from two hooks in the wall.

'There, you won't see much of it now,' he said, gently. 'Perhaps you'll feel better.'

'I c-can't tell you how much I des-despise myself for such w-weakness,' stammered Alethea.

'Why should you? We all have our Achilles' heel. And for a female you are very indomitable, you know. I must confess it's almost a relief to discover that you have some maidenly shrinkings.'

She tried to laugh, but another thunder clap came just then which seemed to shake the whole building. She jumped distractedly to her feet and stood there, white faced and shaking.

For a second he hesitated. Then he placed an arm about her and led her back, unresisting, to the bench. Removing her limp and sodden bonnet and casting it aside, he seated himself beside her and drew her gently towards him so that her head rested on his shoulder. She allowed it to remain there, closing her eyes and giving a fluttering sigh.

'There, now,' he said, in a soothing tone. 'Think that I'm your Papa or one of your brothers, or whoever it is you seek solace from at moments such as this. I undertake not to step out of the role.'

She knew that he spoke the truth, for his enfolding arms, though tender and protective, were not in the least loverlike. In that unexpected haven all her unreasoning fears were stilled. She uttered a deep, heartfelt sigh; relaxed, comforted, no longer conscious of the storm that still raged about them.

They sat there without further speech while the rain beat like drumsticks on the roof of their retreat. Gradually the fury of the storm abated; the lightning became less violent and the thunder rolled away into the distance, until at last it ceased altogether.

She stirred then, raising her head and looking into his eyes. A deep blush spread over her face. At once he removed his arms from about her and rose to his feet.

'It's over now,' he said, in a brisk tone. He moved to the door and flung open the top section. 'The rain will soon be over, too, I believe. We must go up to the house and see if my grandmother can find you some dry garments. I trust you won't take a chill.'

His deliberately matter-of-fact tones helped her to recover her poise. 'Oh, no, I'm not in the least prone to chills. But I don't wish to put Lady Carteret to any trouble —'

He seemed not to hear her. He was leaning on the lower part of the door, gazing out at the rainswept yard. After a moment, he roused himself and went off to speak to the grooms about a conveyance to take her up to the house.

It was almost an hour later that Alethea entered the small salon where Devenish's grandmother was sitting.

'Come and sit here, my dear. I think you'll find this wing chair comfortable,' invited Lady Carteret. 'Did my maid manage to find you something to fit tolerably well? Ah, I see she did — a trifle on the ample side, perhaps, but it will serve you until you reach Roxeth Place, will it not?'

'Thank you, ma'am, indeed it will,' replied Alethea, as she seated herself. 'You are very good, but I must not trespass too long upon your hospitality.'

'At least you'll stay long enough to take a dish of tea,' said Lady Carteret. 'The panacea for all evils, is it not? If you are not too fatigued for talking, perhaps you will like to tell me how you came to be in such a pickle as you were when James found you. How very fortunate that he should have taken the short cut through the wood after seeing that nice Allerton boy a little way on his road home!' She smiled. 'They are all boys to me, you know, Miss Newnham. At my age, it's difficult to remember that the children one knew are now become men and women.'

'So my Papa often says, ma'am,' answered Alethea, glancing covertly around the room as she wondered when Devenish would return, and how she could possibly face him. 'But as for my plight, it was really all my own fault. I was warned that a storm was brewing and not to go far. Indeed, I didn't intend to, but I rode into the wood for shade, and then lost my way, having been so foolish as to dispense with the services of a groom.'

'Well, one can't put old heads on young shoulders, they say; and a very good thing, too, for only think how odd they would look there! I dare say you'll have come to no harm, for you don't look a sickly child — quite the reverse, in fact. And in case anyone should be anxious about you at Roxeth Place, I've sent a message round to reassure them. James will take you back in the carriage presently, when you are sufficiently rested.'

'Oh, no!' exclaimed Alethea, involuntarily. Then, fearing that this sounded uncivil, she added hastily, 'There is really no occasion for Sir James to put himself to so much trouble, ma'am. I can very well go home on Dulcetta, since I see it has quite stopped raining now and the sun is coming out again.'

'And no doubt lose your way once more!' laughed Lady Carteret. 'No, you had far better go in the carriage, and one of the grooms can take the mare.'

'But I assure you, ma'am, that I can't possibly lose myself this time, for I shall keep to the road, and it is no distance at all,' persisted Alethea.

'Well, you must argue the matter with my grandson, for he seems determined to take you back, and I have long since ceased to attempt to tell him what he must do.' Her shrewd eyes, so like Devenish's, searched Alethea's face and saw the embarrassment there. 'What can he have been at to give you a disinclination for his company?' she asked with a laugh.

Alethea blushed faintly. 'It's only that I don't wish to put him to any more trouble on my behalf. He has been to enough already — I feel such a nuisance —'

'You need not, James rarely does anything that he doesn't wish to do. Not that I would have you think him selfish —' She broke off, and her face lit with the fond smile common to grandmothers when speaking of their descendants. 'He's not near such a cold fish as he would have people suppose. He came into his independence young, and he's a dandy, of course, just as his father and grandfather before him — the Devenishes were always men of fashion. But there's more to him than that, as few people realise. At Oxford he was considered quite a prodigious classical scholar, but he was possessed of too lively a temperament to suit the donnish men. In him, the talents are oddly mixed; more so than in most men, who are content to be either one thing or the other.' She sighed. 'And then, of course, there is that quirky sense of humour, which I understand so well because he inherits it from my late husband. Altogether, his is a character which could well be misinterpreted. But there!' She reached out a hand and rested it lightly on Alethea's for a moment. 'I feel I am prosing on in the most boring way about my grandson — a habit of elderly females. Pray forgive me, my dear. Can I offer you some more tea?'

Alethea declined the tea and would have attempted some answer to the rest of the speech, but just then Beau Devenish came into the room. He had changed his damp riding dress for a well-cut coat of light blue over a blue and white striped waistcoat and fawn breeches. She looked up at him, and it was as though a flame sprang up inside her. She quickly removed her gaze to the tea table, and kept it there.

Lady Carteret offered him tea, but he refused and seemed disinclined for conversation; so presently she said that perhaps she ought not to detain Alethea.

'I shall see you tomorrow evening at Lady Middleham's,' she said, as she took Alethea's hand in parting. 'Pray give her my compliments. I trust that she hasn't been made anxious about you, and that you yourself may feel no ill effects.'

Alethea thanked her for her kindness, and went with Devenish to the waiting carriage. During the short drive to Roxeth Place, they had little to say to one another. Once she attempted to thank him, but he dismissed the subject. When they arrived at the house, he escorted her to the door but refused her invitation to enter.

'Take better care of yourself,' he counselled, as they parted, 'for the future.'

He sounded as though he really meant this, thought Alethea, as the door closed upon him. Was it possible — could it be that —? But she shut her mind resolutely to speculation which could only add to her present emotional upheaval.

Chapter XIX

Lydia was still in the doldrums on the following day. Even the prospect of an evening party which would be attended by several unattached young men, failed to raise her spirits. She kept complaining to Alethea that she was bored to death with Roxeth Place, with country society generally and with herself most of all.

'I can't wait to get back to Town,' she concluded, after her second long diatribe in this vein. 'Life here is beyond anything dreary — I only wonder that Eleanor can endure it!'

'You seemed to be enduring it tolerably well before Mr Allerton returned to London,' retorted Alethea, whose patience was understandably wearing a bit thin.

'Why, yes, of course I did! Vivyan is exactly the kind of company I am used to, and most enjoy.'

'And isn't Sir James Devenish in that category?' asked Alethea, forcing herself to speak the name.

Lydia pursed her lips. 'Well, yes, in a way. But he and I are finished — you are the one he is paying attention to now, for the moment at any rate. But, anyway, one cannot compare him to Vivyan, who is the soul of sincerity.'

'You think Sir James could never be sincere?'

'Not he! He has such an odious quizzing sense of humour! Even when he's flirting with one, and paying the most extravagant compliments, somehow one can never quite believe in them. Indeed, I always have the oddest feeling that he is all the time laughing at me! It's not altogether comfortable, I assure you, and I'm not at all sorry to be quit of him. But Vivyan —' her face softened — 'Oh, he's quite different.'

Alethea considered her cousin thoughtfully. 'I wonder, Lydia, if you don't perhaps mistake your interest in Mr Allerton.'

'Mistake? What can you mean?'

'It's none of my business, of course; but I think you believe yourself to be merely indulging in a flirtation with him, do you not?'

Lydia studied her fingernails for a moment in silence. 'Well — yes —'

'Forgive me,' said Alethea, quietly, 'but — are you quite sure that you're not more deeply involved? During the time we've been together, I've come to know you fairly well, and it does seem to me that he means more to you than any other gentleman whom I've seen in your company.'

There was no sound in the room for several minutes but the ticking of the ormolu clock on the mantelshelf. Lydia sat perfectly still, staring into space.

Suddenly the tears were falling down her face.

'Oh, what can I do, Alethea?'

Alethea shook her head. 'I can't advise you, my dear. You're the best judge of how matters stand.'

'Mama!' sobbed Lydia. 'And Bedwyn! It's true what Mama says, it would be a splendid match — I would like to be a Duchess — well, who wouldn't, pray? But — but — Vivyan —'

Her grief exploded on the final word. She buried her face in her hands while sobs shook her whole body. Alethea rose quickly and went over to her, putting an arm about her shoulders.

'There, there,' she soothed. 'You mustn't upset yourself so. Only wait until you feel calmer, and then you can perhaps consider what it is you most want.'

Lydia made no reply, but clung to her cousin until the storm of weeping was over. Then she began to dry her eyes.

'Tell me what you would do in my place,' she asked, tremulously.

'I can only suppose what I'd do if I were still myself, and I don't think that would help you very much. We're such very different people.'

'I expect you'll say that you would refuse Bedwyn and marry Vivyan,' said Lydia, half defiantly.

'If I truly loved Mr Allerton, yes. It wouldn't cross my mind to accept anyone else. But then I'm not you, and I've never wished to be a Duchess, nor make a brilliant match. So how can I possibly say how you ought to act?'

'You're always so *rational*, Alethea! Don't you ever find yourself in a turmoil, pulled this way and that by conflicting feelings, so that for the life of you, you can't tell what you should do?'

'Not very often, thank goodness, though I suppose everyone does at some time or another. But I have a profound distrust of taking any important decision when one is in a highly emotional state, so the only advice I will give you is to defer yours for a little while.'

Lydia nodded, and no more was said between them on the subject. Alethea reflected wryly that, if only Lydia had known it, her own emotions were in a scarcely less chaotic state than her cousin's. She found herself at once dreading and longing for the inevitable meeting with Beau Devenish at the party that evening.

In the event, there seemed to be very little opportunity for private conversation between them. About twenty people were present, judiciously mixed as to age and sex. After dinner was over, the older members of the party played cards while the younger ones entertained themselves with conversation, music and an impromptu country dance.

During the meal, Devenish had been seated at some distance from Alethea, and, after it was over, he seemed in no hurry to seek her company. When they did chance to be together for a few moments from time to time, he had nothing to say that was in any way personal. He made no reference to yesterday's encounter beyond expressing a hope that her health was none the worse for it, and conveying a similar message from Lady Carteret. Not once did he make any attempt to pay her one of his lighthearted compliments, or flirt with her in the old way. Alethea tried to tell herself that his changed conduct was a great relief to her; but she was too honest to succeed in this, and had to acknowledge her disappointment. Yesterday, they had seemed to be so close. She had wanted that new intimacy and understanding to continue and ripen. Her heart sank as she realised the full implications of this desire. It seemed she was in no better plight than Lydia.

She had too much pride to let anyone else suspect her feelings, however, and a lifelong habit of self-control helped her to mask them. She chatted pleasantly to the rest of the party, took her turn at the pianoforte and joined in the dancing with as much zest as anyone present. Once when she was being partnered by an agreeable young man who had shown her a certain amount of attention throughout the evening, she noticed Devenish's eye upon her. He was frowning; but as soon as he saw that her head was turned in his direction, he looked away, addressing some remark to the young lady with whom he was dancing at that moment. He did not once partner Alethea; but this might have been due to the impromptu nature of the dancing, with every man leading in whichever young lady happened to be nearest to him at the time.

Alethea was relieved to see that Lydia seemed to have thrown off her despondent mood and throughout the evening had been ready to smile on every gentleman who showed a tendency to admire her. As usual, there were several of these, and it was some time before Devenish came close enough to her to exchange a few words.

'When do you return to Town?' she asked him.

'Tomorrow. I collect you and Miss Newnham leave here on the following day?'

She nodded. 'And not a day too soon for me, I assure you! Indeed, I wish we could return tomorrow, too, but Mama would not hear of Sunday travelling, of course.'

'No, it's only for unregenerate characters like myself,' he agreed, with a lazy smile. 'But don't you care for a country life, Miss Lydia? The beauties of nature leave you unmoved? I suppose that is because you have beauty enough in your own person.'

'Humbug!' She could not resist giving him an arch smile, though the old conviction was lacking. 'Don't think to take me in, sir, with your compliments! You have no eyes for me nowadays — it is my cousin to whom you should be addressing such remarks!'

'To your cousin — Miss Newnham, do you mean?'

'What other cousins have I present, pray? You know quite well whom I mean, so it's of no use to dissemble.'

'Alas,' he drawled, 'I fear my poor compliments give scant pleasure to Miss Newnham. She will have none of them.'

'And who is to blame for that, pray? The reason isn't far to seek — she knows very well how little you mean what you say!'

'Our acquaintance is so slight that Miss Newnham cannot know anything of me at all.'

'Don't depend upon that, sir!' She fluttered her fan at him in reproof. 'We poor females must look out for ourselves, you know, where you scheming gentlemen are concerned; and there are plenty of us to warn her what an odiously wretched flirt you are, and how little to be believed!'

His smile lingered as though fixed. 'I see. Do I collect that you have already given your cousin such a warning?'

'Why, of course! I should be totally lacking in all family feeling did I allow her to become an easy prey to one of the most accomplished philanderers in Town! I could never forgive myself!'

'How very thoughtful of you, Miss Lydia. And I make no doubt that you show a similar compassion towards your own victims?' There was a hint of steel behind the indolent charm of his voice. 'You would always make it quite clear to them that you were not in earnest, and it was all a game?'

She could scarcely mistake his meaning. Two spots of colour showed in her cheeks.

'Bah!' she exclaimed disdainfully. 'What an odious wretch you can be at times!'

He bowed. 'As you say, ma'am. And I suppose that being so, I cannot persuade you to stand up with me in this next dance?'

'Certainly not — in any case, I promised it to Mr Mainwaring. See, here he comes. Not that one needs to preserve strict etiquette at a scrambling affair such as this,' she added, to give point to her rejection of him.

His smile widened, showing genuine amusement.

'No, only when it chances to suit one's inclinations,' he agreed, affably.

She made no answer to this, but turned her sweetest smile on Mr Mainwaring, who promptly led her into the set that was forming. Devenish did his duty by another young lady who wished to take part; but from time to time his glance flickered towards the pianoforte, where Alethea was taking her turn at providing the music. So she had been warned off him, had she? It was something he might have expected, and perhaps it accounted in part for his total lack of success in getting up a flirtation with her. But that failure no longer rankled, for now his ambitions had changed.

Chapter XX

Eleanor saw the two girls off on Monday with many expressions of regret for the shortness of their visit.

'You must come again after my confinement,' she said to Lydia. 'I can't tell you how much good it has done me to have you here — I was feeling so downcast and dreary, and now I'm quite in spirits again! You, too, Alethea — next time you need a change from Somerset, pray do come and spend a few weeks with us. Dulcetta and the children will miss you sadly, too.'

'Well, for my part,' said Lydia to her cousin, as they settled themselves in the coach and set off for the road to London, 'I shan't be in a hurry to return to Harrow. I like to see Eleanor now and then, of course, but a few days of the country lasts me for a very long time. It will be better when she can come up to Town to pay us a visit.'

'But I fail to see what is so very different about life in your sister's home,' objected Alethea. 'We were entertained in much the same way as we would have been in London — evening parties and the like. We even had the company of two gentlemen from among your London acquaintances.'

Lydia frowned. 'Yes, that's the one thing that worries me, Alethea. If Mama should discover that Vivyan was there, there will be serious trouble, for she sent me away on purpose to separate us, as you well know. Do you think you could possibly avoid mentioning his name? Or Devenish's, too, come to think of it, for if we speak of him it will lead on naturally to Vivyan.'

Alethea looked dubious. 'I'm such an unconvincing liar,' she protested. 'And, in any event, won't your sister write and tell my Aunt all about it? Unless you swore her to secrecy, of course.'

'No such thing! To do that would have been to invite her to tell Mama the whole! No, I am hoping that she won't write for a day or two, and perhaps by then it won't very much matter. Mama may have something else to think about.'

'You mean perhaps the preparations for the ball on Thursday?'

'Not precisely the preparations, but I was thinking of the ball. You know Bedwyn is to be present.' She paused a moment, then added, 'If I play my cards aright I can most likely bring him to a declaration. After that, Mama is not going to worry about Vivyan any more.'

Alethea considered her cousin thoughtfully. 'I see. Does this mean that you have decided to accept the Duke?'

Lydia raised her chin defiantly. 'Yes. I followed your advice, Alethea, and waited until I felt rational enough to weigh one thing against another. And it came to me at the party last night that all I needed to keep me content was to have plenty of admirers around me and to be a lady of consequence. Another thing, Bedwyn is quite old, you know and may leave me a rich widow before long.'

'It's melancholy indeed to think that you're looking forward to being a widow before you're a wife,' said Alethea. 'Are you quite sure that you can face the interim period with equanimity?'

'Why not? Lots of girls marry men whom they scarce know or even like — men chosen for them by their parents. It seems to answer well enough for them, so why not for me?'

'What about your sister Caroline? Would you say a marriage of convenience has answered for her?'

Lydia shrugged. 'Caro's was not near such a brilliant match as mine would be. Besides, her case was different — she was madly in love with another man when she was persuaded to accept Fothergill.'

'And you are not?' asked Alethea, bluntly.

'Oh, I have a tendre for Vivyan, I admit; but I expect I shall recover from it, like the measles,' replied Lydia, airily.

'As long as you are certain.' Alethea said no more, but stared out of the window at the fields and hedges slowly slipping past. Lydia picked up a copy of the Lady's Magazine which she had brought with her, and soon appeared to be immersed in its pages. When she did speak again presently, it was to ask Alethea's opinion on the style of a gown described there.

Evidently the previous topic was at an end.

As things turned out, it was quite easy to avoid any mention of Devenish or Allerton, because Mrs Manbury's questions about their visit were solely concerned with her daughter Eleanor and the two grandchildren. Having satisfied herself that they were all well, she quickly changed the conversation to the arrangements for the forthcoming ball. It was quite a relief to Alethea to be able to escape from endless discussions on this subject for one evening at least when on the following day she attended the soiree at Montagu House with Miss Hannah More.

She was again received by Mrs Montagu with great kindness. The room was very full of company and they had some difficulty in finding seats; but two gentlemen made way for them, and they were soon drawn into a group surrounding a very lively lady whom Miss More introduced as Mrs Vesey.

'She is a particular friend of Mrs Montagu's,' Miss More explained to Alethea in an aside, 'and gives similar parties herself. They call her "The Sylph", but I cannot think such a nickname altogether suitable for one who is the wife of an M.P. and the daughter of a Bishop.'

But Alethea was far too interested in the conversation which was going on in the circle surrounding Mrs Vesey, to trouble her head about such a triviality as the lady's nickname.

She became so deeply absorbed that a light touch on her arm made her jump. Turning, she saw Elizabeth Montagu standing there with a younger lady at her side. Alethea rose at once, and to her delight found herself being presented to Miss Frances Burney, the celebrated authoress of *Evelina* and *Cecilia*.

'Miss Newnham is perhaps in something the same situation as your heroine in *Evelina*,' said Mrs Montagu to Fanny Burney, with a smile. 'She, too, is being introduced into the Polite World after having been brought up in the country. On that account, I am sure I can recommend her to your kindness.'

She then thoughtfully drew Miss More away with her to another part of the room, so that Alethea could enjoy a few moments alone with the novelist.

It was quite a surprise to Alethea to find that such a well-known author, who had been lionised by society in general and made much of by eminent figures such as Dr Johnson and Edmund Burke, should be so modest and retiring by nature. Miss Burney seemed reluctant to talk about her writing at all; but gradually she responded to Alethea's intelligent, informed interest, so much more to her taste than the fulsome extravagant praise to which she was so often subjected by people who had only skimmed through her books because it was the fashion to have read them.

'You must have been beyond anything elated when you knew, ma'am, that your novel was accepted for publication,' said Alethea after a time.

'You may not credit it, Miss Newnham, but I was at once elated and terrified! I hardly knew how to believe it real; and when I succeeded in convincing myself that it was indeed so, and that my poor scribblings were to be offered to the world, terror was the predominant sensation I experienced.'

'Yes,' replied Alethea, 'I think I can understand that. You must have felt rather like a mother exposing her new-born infant naked on a mountain top.'

'Exactly so! From the first, I always felt that my writing was an unworthy pastime. I strove to keep it a secret, and only my sister Susan was allowed to share in it. Indeed, when I was fifteen years old, I made a bonfire of everything I had so far written.'

'Oh, what a shame! But I can perfectly comprehend your feelings — you were too modest.'

Miss Burney shook her head. 'I always had a horror of exposing my work to the critical gaze of others. I wrote *Evelina* without any notion of publication, solely for my own private recreation. It was my brother Charles who persuaded me to try and get it into print. I only agreed for a frolic, for I was curious to see how a production of my very own would look in that author-like form. I insisted, though, that it should be offered to a publisher anonymously. And I did not even let my own father into the secret!'

'But he would know about it eventually, of course. Was he as pleased with it as all the rest of the world, ma'am?'

'Yes, he saw a review of it in the periodical *Monthly Review*, and at once sent round to the publisher's for the book. I was so relieved when he told me that he had read it, and I need not blush for it — his praise I value far beyond that of the professional critics.' She broke off as Miss More came to rejoin them. 'But I must not fatigue you, Miss Newnham, with such talk. There must be many other people here whom you are desirous of meeting.'

'On the contrary, Miss Burney, meeting you has been an event for which I scarcely dared to hope, and one which will be envied me by all my friends, I assure you.'

They exchanged bows and parted. Alethea, her face pink with pleasure, turned to Miss More.

'Who would suppose, ma'am, that such a celebrated authoress would be so modest and unassuming? I had the utmost difficulty in persuading her to speak to me of her work, but I am beyond anything glad that I managed it at last. Only wait until I tell them at home — they will be envying me prodigiously!'

It was while the refreshments were being served that Mr Tracy appeared at Alethea's side.

'Have you been here long, ladies?' he asked. 'I — um — have been watching out for you, but — er — um — there is quite a large company here this evening, is there not?'

He gave the apologetic little laugh which always made Alethea feel sorry for him. It must be a great trial to be so shy, she thought, and she could not help contrasting him with Devenish, just for a moment. Then she resolutely closed her mind to such thoughts and set out as usual to put him a little more at his ease, so that he might do justice to himself in conversation. She told him that she had been fortunate enough to speak with Miss Burney, and this led on to a discussion of the merits of her novel *Evelina*.

'As to novels in general,' remarked Hannah More, 'one cannot wholly approve the reading of them as a rational occupation for young, unformed minds. But the high moral tone of Miss Burney's novels must exempt them from this criticism. A young girl who models her conduct on that of Eveline cannot but find benefit.'

'No, indeed, ma'am,' agreed Alethea, 'for I can't help feeling that at times Miss Burney's heroine is almost too good to be true. She is exceptionally beautiful, virtuous, dutiful and compassionate — a model of all a young female ought to be. I must say, the mere notion of trying to emulate her example casts me into a fit of the dismals, for I know I can never succeed!'

Miss More gave an austere smile. 'Well, my sisters tell me you had always a lively wit, Alethea, so I know better than to take what you say in earnest. But I would not like to think that you are giving a false impression of your character to Mr Tracy.'

'Um — as to that, Miss More,' stuttered Tracy, 'Assure you — um — er — nothing Miss Newnham says can — um — in any way — er — alter the very high esteem — um — in which I hold her.'

His earnest look as he said this made Alethea feel a little uncomfortable; and she was not sorry when some other people joined in their discussion, which gradually drifted on to other literary topics. He remained at their side, though, throughout the remainder of the evening, leaving when they left, and attending them to their carriage.

'We shall — er — meet again, Miss Newnham, at your — um — at Mrs Manbury's ball on Thursday,' he said, in parting. 'I am — um — not much of a dancing man, but — er — um — will esteem it a great favour if you — er — will be so good as to — um — reserve me a dance, ma'am?'

Alethea promised, wondering as she did so if on this occasion she might be asked to dance by Devenish.

Chapter XXI

Thursday was a day of great activity in Curzon Street, with tradesmen coming and going busy delivering goods to Mrs Manbury's house. Long before noon, a red carpet had been laid down the steps and an awning erected which extended from the front door to the street. Inside the house, the staff worked in an atmosphere of organised bustle. Those who had been responsible for making ready the ballroom stood waiting with bated breath while the butler slowly surveyed the results of their labours with a keenly critical eye. A combination of polish and elbow-grease had brought the floor to such a state of perfection that the three handsome chandeliers suspended above it, their lustres gleaming, were plainly mirrored in its surface; hangings, cheval glasses, chairs and sofas all reached the same high standard. He nodded austerely, satisfied, and a sigh of relief went up from his minions.

Mrs Manbury was occupied in carrying out an inspection of her own in Alethea's bedchamber. Her eyes showed warm approval as they rested on the gown of cream silk which so well set off her niece's fair skin and the brown hair burnished with red-gold tints, which was dressed with one large ringlet falling on her neck. The only jewellery Alethea wore was a pair of dangling earrings in amethyst and pearl; this, too, her Aunt approved, as she considered it in bad taste for a young girl to be loaded down with jewels.

'You look charmingly, my dear,' she said, pleased.

Lydia, who was looking as bewitching as ever in a gown of buttercup yellow trimmed with white, also added her tribute to this; and Mrs Manbury, well satisfied with the appearance of both her charges, led them to join her husband at the reception area.

Receiving the guests was a long and tedious business, thought Alethea, who did not know very many of them. The Allertons arrived early in the proceedings; Alethea noticed that although Vivyan Allerton gave her cousin an eloquent glance as he bowed over her hand, Lydia herself was several degrees cooler towards him than of late. Evidently this did not escape him, either, for he frowned, as he passed on into the room with the rest of his family, continuing to look back at intervals as though he would dearly have liked to be able to have a private word with her.

The Allertons were followed by a great many people whom Alethea did not know; so it was with some relief that she recognised Mr Tracy hovering on the threshold, looking as if he almost wished he had not come. She bestowed an especially warm smile on him in an endeavour to cheer him up, then turned away to discover that the next person waiting to greet her was Beau Devenish.

She caught her breath. He looked so very handsome in his coat of crimson and white striped taffeta; his carriage was so assured, his bow so graceful, that a comparison with Paul Tracy was inevitable. She wrestled with her feelings to such good effect that she managed to produce for him a polite, cool smile in direct contrast to the one with which Devenish had just seen her distinguish the poet. A half-rueful, half-amused expression came into his eyes as he walked away to join the rest of the company in the room.

Arrivals now came thick and fast. From time to time, Mrs Manbury confided to her husband's reluctant ear her misgivings as to whether the Duke of Bedwyn would come or not. She had almost given up hope and Mr Manbury had nearly lost all patience, when the long-expected name was announced and the Duke was making his bow to them.

Alethea's eyes at once turned towards him in lively curiosity, for she had heard so much talk of this nobleman that she could scarcely wait to see what kind of husband her cousin had chosen. He was a short, portly man well into his sixties with a florid complexion which the puce coat he was wearing only served to accentuate. He was fashionably dressed and had an air of consequence consistent with his rank; but Alethea, watching his proprietorial air as he greeted her cousin, suddenly felt deeply sorry for Lydia. To choose such a man instead of Vivyan Allerton — surely it was an impossibility?

The Duke remained at Lydia's side until the reception party dispersed, and then led her into the first dance, a country dance of the longways progressive style. As Alethea herself was partnered by her cousin Caroline's husband, George Fothergill, no great demands were made on her conversational powers, so she was at liberty to observe the other dancers. She noticed that Allerton had at first hung back, obviously wanting to approach Lydia; but when he saw Bedwyn take her on to the floor, he turned away as if unwilling to dance at all before recollecting himself and leading out a young lady in pink who was chatting to his sister Clarinda. And very heavy going he seemed to be making of it, thought Alethea, as she watched the false starts he made from time to time because his attention was fixed on Lydia and her partner rather than on his own movements.

As soon as the dance was over, he started across the room towards the Manburys' party; but by the time he had reached Lydia's side, she had already engaged herself for half the evening. Alethea was close by and heard her cousin tell him so with a regret that was patently insincere.

'I can save you the cotillion before supper,' Lydia offered, in a tone of indifference.

'Not until then?' he asked, in some indignation. 'Egad, Lydia, I would have thought you might have reserved an earlier one for me!'

She gave an affected laugh, 'You forget, Vivyan, that we are such old friends people think of us as brother and sister; and it does not do to be dancing with one's brother when there are other gentlemen in the room wishing to partner one, does it?'

He stared at her for a moment as if he had been struck in the face. Under his scrutiny, Lydia reddened slightly. Then he gave a stiff little bow.

'Very well, then, madam, keep me the cotillion, if you please.'

He turned on his heel, almost falling over Devenish, who had come up behind him. He apologised brusquely and passed on, ignoring his friend completely.

'Dear me, it would seem that Allerton is in the deuce of a hurry,' remarked Devenish to the two girls. 'Can it be that one of you ladies is in urgent need of refreshment? Or possibly both? Though after only one dance such an eventuality would appear unlikely.'

Lydia shrugged and attempted a nonchalant smile. 'Oh, he's gone off in a miff,' she said, carelessly, 'because I'm engaged for the next few dances. It's of no consequence — he'll soon get over it.'

Beau Devenish put up his quizzing glass and surveyed her through it for a moment with a mocking glance. 'I wonder? But you must allow me to compliment both you ladies on your looks tonight. I dare say many a man present will feel chagrined if he must wait too long before being able to have the inestimable pleasure of leading you out. I take it that there is no hope for me at present, then? Doubtless you are both engaged until after supper? Possibly, even, for the rest of the evening?'

He addressed them both equally, with no special look or smile for Alethea. Her heart sank, and her answering smile felt rigid, as though glued to her face. She told herself severely that she had been hoping too much, expecting too much from what had gone before. Why must she be so foolish? The man was a flirt of the most accomplished kind — everyone had told her so, and there had been ample opportunity for her to confirm it for herself. Only, there had been a few moments on the day of the thunderstorm, when she had caught a glimpse, or so it seemed at the time, of a vastly different Beau Devenish.

She was about to tell him untruthfully that he had guessed aright and that she was indeed engaged for the entire evening, but Lydia forestalled her.

'Oh, you must certainly dance with my cousin, for the ball is in her honour,' she said. 'I believe she promised the next dance to Mr Tracy, did you not, Alethea? But I dare say she can manage to squeeze you in somewhere,' she added, condescendingly.

Devenish's lips twitched at this blatant set-down, but he applied gravely enough to Alethea for the favour. Although she despised herself for her weakness, she found she was unable to refuse him altogether, and promised him the dance after Paul Tracy's.

She was soon to discover that when Paul Tracy had told her he was not much of a dancing man, he had not been over modest. His steps were scarcely less halting than his speech, with the result that the other dancers on the floor were constantly having their movements impeded by his awkwardness. Alethea did her best not to appear put out by his mistakes; but the consciousness of Beau Devenish's eye upon her from his place in the set close by, did succeed in bringing a little colour of embarrassment to her cheeks. The worst moment came when Mr Tracy trod on the hem of her gown. Fortunately, it did not tear; but the accident threw them so completely out of step that they were forced to retire from the set.

To avoid crossing the room while the dance was in progress, they made their way to a sofa in an alcove, and here they sat while Alethea listened to Paul Tracy's profuse apologies. She tried her best to reassure him; no harm had been done to her gown, and he was to think nothing of it.

'But — um — er —' he stuttered helplessly, 'I cannot help — um — feeling — er — deeply distressed. To — to appear so f-foolish, so maladroit — um — er — to you, of all people! To you, to — to whom I — um — er — would wish to — to appear in — um — er — the most favourable l-light — um — possible!'

Alethea looked at him in dismay. All too well she saw what was coming, and did her best to avert it; first of all by laughing the incident off, and then, when that failed, by trying to introduce another subject. All her efforts were in vain, however. Made bold by desperation, Mr Tracy seized her hand and poured out a halting, though affecting, avowal of love. In spite of his unfortunate impediment, his command of words was such that she could not remain totally unaffected, even if her compassion had not been touched by his obvious sincerity. Tears came to her eyes as she drew away her hand and explained gently that she was quite unable to reciprocate his feelings.

'Time,' he said, urgently. 'Of — of course you need more time. I — I have — um — been too sudden — er — too ill-advised —'

As compassionately but as firmly as she was able, she set herself to dispel any hopes of this kind he might be nursing. He was too sincere a man not to be answered with complete honesty, and she knew now that her heart was irrevocably given elsewhere. As she finished speaking, she looked up and saw that Devenish was watching them from his place among the dancers. It was too much. She felt her composure cracking; and excusing herself somewhat incoherently to her companion, made her way out of the room and rushed to the seclusion of her bedchamber.

Once there, she flung herself face down on the bed and gave way to the tears which threatened to choke her.

A few minutes unrestrained sobbing was sufficient to bring relief. She raised herself on one elbow and groped for a pocket handkerchief. As she did so, she heard someone enter the room; turning her head, she saw Lydia there.

'Alethea, my dear!' Her cousin came to sit beside her on the bed and stroked her hair with unwonted tenderness. 'What is it? I saw you go, and guessed there must be something amiss — was it something to do with Mr Tracy?'

Alethea nodded and sat up, drying her eyes. 'Yes — he — he made me a declaration,' she replied, unsteadily.

'I thought it might be that, for I could see he was speaking very earnestly to you. Did you accept him?'

Alethea shook her head.

'No?' Lydia sounded incredulous. 'Oh, but I dare say you will do, when you've had time to get used to the idea. He is quite a good match, you know, and I must say you are better suited to each other than most people. I dare say he took you unawares — such things can often come as a shock.'

175

Alethea stood up and went over to the washstand. She poured some water from a jug into the basin and bathed her face.

'You mistake, Lydia,' she said, as she dried herself. 'I can never marry Mr Tracy.'

'Lud, you sound very sure of yourself! I tell you what, Mama will be no end put out if you do not — she's quite counting on it.'

'This is a matter in which I can allow no one else to guide me.'

She had quite recovered now and her voice was firm. She smoothed her gown, patted her hair into place before the mirror, then turned to her cousin.

'Shall we go back to the ballroom?'

'Yes, if you're quite ready.' Lydia rose from the bed. 'But, Alethea —' she hesitated a moment — 'it's not because of Devenish, is it?'

She eyed Alethea keenly as she spoke, and did not miss the tell-tale blush that came before a vigorous shake of the head.

'Well, I'm monstrous glad of it, for he's not serious you know, whatever he may try to make you believe. Vivyan mentioned to me something Devenish once said — I dare say Viv would never have repeated it, but that he thought I ought to give you a warning. It seems Devenish told Vivyan that his only interest in you was as a quarry which seemed to be eluding his grasp. Those were his exact words, Alethea. I'm sorry.'

'You need not be,' replied Alethea, in a tight little voice. 'I'm not so gullible as to think otherwise. Say no more about it — let us go back.'

They reached the ballroom just as the set for the next dance was forming. Lydia was whisked off at once by an anxious partner who had feared that she was trying to evade her engagement to dance with him. Devenish presented himself in more leisurely fashion to lead Alethea out on to the floor.

She was quite sure that by now she had her feelings well in control. She would not betray herself by one look or word, but would behave towards him as she would do any other gentleman who might happen to dance with her that evening. She would be polite but cool, talk no more than was necessary and keep to generalities.

But one touch of his hand put her emotions in such a turmoil that all her good resolutions melted away like ice in the sun. He looked down at her; there was no trace of the usual mockery in those hazel eyes, but a deep tenderness which she could have sworn was genuine. Their eyes met and held for a moment, and she saw the tightening of a muscle in his cheek. Her heart leapt. Could it be — was it possible that he, too, was struggling to keep equally powerful emotions in control? Or did she think so only because she longed with all her heart to believe it true? Was she deluding herself?

Suddenly she was weary of fighting this losing battle with her feelings; for this one dance she told herself she would surrender completely to the illusion of being loved as she had come to love. After that, she would face the truth with what courage she could muster.

For a while they did not speak at all as they followed the movements of the dance, now taking them apart from each other, now bringing them together again. It was no awkward silence, however, but one that to Alethea seemed to arise from the sense of feelings between them which lay too deep for words. At last, during a figure which kept them together for rather longer than usual, he spoke.

'I trust your late partner did not tear your gown, Miss Newnham. I saw that he was so clumsy as to step on it.'

'Oh, no.' Her voice was a little breathless. 'No damage was done, fortunately.'

'I did wonder, since you left the ballroom somewhat abruptly not long afterwards,' he continued looking at her searchingly. 'I thought you seemed a trifle discomposed?'

She made no answer, uncertain what to say.

'Forgive me,' he said, with no trace of his usual drawl. 'My remarks must seem impertinent to you — indeed, they would be in any ordinary circumstances, but I have reason —'

She shook her head, too overcome for words.

'Even at the risk of further incurring your displeasure,' he went on, hurriedly, 'I must finish what I have to say. It appeared to me that Mr Tracy was speaking to you in a very particular fashion, and that you — though I may be quite mistaken in this — were distressed by his behaviour. Good God, I don't mind admitting that I could have run him through on the spot had that been possible!'

The vehemence of his tone added to the unexpectedness of what he had said shook Alethea considerably, and it was as well that the figures of the dance at that point required them to separate for some time.

At first, her thoughts were in a turmoil. Could he really be in earnest — was it at all possible? She knew that he had been observing her closely while she had been in Mr Tracy's company. Now he had spoken like a man in the grip of jealousy. Could it be so?

But gradually, as she found herself obliged to answer a succession of trivial remarks made to her by the other dancers in the set, her racing thoughts steadied and doubts set in. She told herself that what she would like to think of as the jealousy of a man in love might equally well — and much more likely, in this case — be the chagrin of a determined flirt who sees another about to succeed where he has failed. She recalled the words repeated to her by Lydia not half an hour since, words attributed to Devenish by Mr Allerton, who surely was not the man to lie about such a matter — 'a quarry eluding his grasp'. They were burnt on her mind in letters of fire.

With all the strength of her being, she wanted to think him loving, tender, sincere; but though she had surrendered her heart too readily, she must not completely lose her head. All the evidence at her disposal pointed to the unwelcome fact that he was merely trifling with her. Well, he had succeeded in storming the citadel; but at least, she determined desperately, he should not be given the satisfaction of knowing as much.

He took her hand when they at last came together again, saying in a low tone, 'Am I forgiven, or are you seriously displeased with me?'

'How could I be displeased with you after the service you rendered me in Harrow?' she replied, as casually as she was able.

'Service — bah! Would I had the right to —'

They were forced to move away from each other again for a moment.

'Confound it!' he exclaimed in exasperation, when he rejoined her. 'This is altogether intolerable — how am I to explain myself in such conditions? Miss Newnham — Alethea —' her heart bounded at the name — 'Give me leave to wait upon you tomorrow. Only name an hour, and I will be there.'

She shook her head. 'I think you had much better not come, Sir James.'

'Not come?' He gripped her hand hard, almost causing her to lose her step, and turned an intense look on her which made her lower her eyes. 'Alethea, look at me! Do you really mean that?'

Keeping all expression out of her face, she forced herself to meet his gaze for a brief moment.

'Yes, I do,' she answered, lifelessly.

He said nothing, and for some time they danced together without speaking.

'I understand you, I suppose,' he said, brusquely. 'Tracy is fortunate indeed. Forgive my importunity.'

She did not correct his mistaken impression. Better that he should believe her affianced to Paul Tracy, for then he would pester her no more with insincere compliments and false protestations. They finished the dance in silence, and parted.

But Alethea felt as though she had died, and only her pale ghost continued to move about amid all the colour and gaiety of the ballroom.

Chapter XXII

After he had left her, Devenish made his way to the refreshment room. He found Vivyan Allerton there, drinking steadily, and frowned, momentarily shaken out of his own gloomy reflections.

'Nothing better to do, Viv?' he demanded as he took a glass of wine from one of the waiters.

Allerton looked up, a heavy scowl on his usually good-tempered face. 'Oh, it's you, is it?'

'None other,' agreed Devenish. 'Wishing me at the devil, are you?'

'Not particularly — there's only one fellow I heartily wish at the devil, and I dare say it don't take three guesses to find out who he is.'

'No,' said Devenish, sipping his wine.

Allerton drained his glass at a gulp and refilled it from a bottle by his elbow. 'For two pins,' he muttered, between clenched teeth, 'I'd call the swine out!'

'Don't chance to have two pins about me. Just as well. You couldn't call him out for two good reasons — one, he's old enough to be your father, and two, it would make a rare scandal!'

'Hell and the devil, don't you think I know that? What am I supposed to do? Stand by while the only girl I ever cared for — ever could care for! — is pushed into marriage with that — doddering old fool!'

Devenish looked quickly about them, but only a few people were in the room and none close enough to overhear.

'You've got it wrong, Viv. I'd say myself that she goes willingly enough.'

For a moment it looked as though Allerton would dash the contents of his glass in the other man's face. Then he controlled himself with an effort, setting the glass down on the table with a shaking hand. When he turned towards Devenish again, the angry expression had been replaced by one of bewilderment.

'But why, James, for God's sake why? You saw her with me at Harrow — tell me honestly, wouldn't you have said she was beginning to care for me at last? I thought so, and God knows I'm no coxcomb — you know that, James!'

'Indeed I do. And I must admit that the lady did seem to be more sincere than I've ever known her to be with anyone else. But I fear you must allow for the influence of her surroundings — away from her matchmaking Mama and the glitter of Town life, no doubt things appeared very differently to her. Now she's back in London, all that has vanished.'

Allerton stared at him in silence for several moments.

'So,' he said at last, slowly, 'what you're saying is that I was no more than a passing interest, a diversion to help relieve the tedium of an enforced stay in the country. Is that it?'

Devenish hesitated. 'I could be wrong, Vivyan, but so it seemed to me.'

'Then by God!' declared Allerton, thrusting out his jaw. 'I'll waste no more time in regretting her! There are pretty girls in plenty out there —' he gestured towards the ballroom — 'so let's go and dance with 'em!'

Although Devenish signified his approval of this, he did not himself stay for more than one dance before making his excuses to his hostess and departing. Allerton, however, went through every dance with a different — and most attractive —

partner, until the time came for his promised cotillion with Lydia. He arrived at her side a few minutes late, on account of an absorbing conversation which he had been holding not two yards away with a pretty young lady in blue from whom he seemed reluctant to part. A tinge of colour crept into Lydia's cheeks as he apologised and hurried her on to the floor. Throughout the dance, he almost ignored his own partner while carrying on a lively flirtation with two of the other young ladies in the set. The cotillion over, he sketched a careless bow to Lydia and hastened to claim one of these young ladies, a vivacious blonde with very free manners, as a supper partner.

The Duke of Bedwyn, who had already danced twice with Lydia, now came to lead her in to supper. He was received with very much less animation than she had so far shown him, and as the meal progressed he had difficulty in forcing a single word out of her. This was made more noticeable by the flow of easy talk and laughter which surrounded them; especially from the opposite side of the table where Allerton had seated himself with his blonde companion and one or two of his cronies. Towards the end of the meal, Allerton started feeding his lively partner with sugar plums by tilting back her head and dropping them into her open mouth. This caused a great deal of mirth amongst her companions, and Lydia suddenly pushed back her chair with an expression of distaste on her face. The Duke came to his feet, assisting her to rise; but as they walked away, Allerton's laughter, seeming to mock, followed them down the room.

When at last the ball came to an end and all their guests had departed, Mrs Manbury flopped wearily into the chair.

'My poor feet!' she moaned. 'They're killing me, I declare! These shoes are monstrous tight — only wait until I see that wretched shoemaker!' She paused to massage her instep, then turned to Lydia. 'One thing I *must* know before I seek my bed — did Bedwyn come to the point?'

'No,' said Lydia shortly.

'There!' exclaimed Mrs Manbury to her husband. 'It's just as I feared — didn't I tell you I'd observed a change in him after supper? Pray, whatever was amiss, Lydia? You were going on famously at first — he was all smiles and attention, you looked charmingly and seemed to be enjoying yourself! — I made quite sure that he would declare himself long before the ball was over, and be waiting upon us during the course of the next few days! I tell you what, Miss, you must have played your cards monstrous badly, for I never saw a man so smitten in my life!'

Lydia made no reply, but burst into tears.

'There, there!' said her father, patting her shoulder soothingly. 'Let be, Olivia — the child's too fatigued to discuss anything now. Indeed, I think we all are. Go to your bed, Lyddy, and everything will look better when you've rested.'

Even his wife saw the value of this advice, so nothing more was said and the family retired for what was left of the night. But as Alethea was wearily undressing, having dismissed her heavy-eyed maid, a faint tap on the door roused her from her unhappy thoughts. Slipping into a dressing gown, she opened the door to find Lydia, still fully dressed, standing outside.

Her cousin said nothing, but stood there with such a hopeless, lost expression on her face, which was ravaged by tears, that Alethea almost burst into tears herself. Taking Lydia's cold hands in hers, she drew her into the room and, quietly shutting the door, led her to a chair.

'What is it, love?' she asked, gently.

Lydia's uncertain composure broke at the tender tone, and for a time both cousins wept in each other's arms.

Alethea recovered first. Disengaging herself and drying her eyes, she went to a drawer and came back with a handkerchief which she gave to Lydia.

'There, we'll both feel better now,' she whispered. 'Can you tell me about it, do you suppose?'

Lydia began to talk, somewhat incoherently at first, her words punctuated by sobs; but the gist of what she said was that she could never, never marry Bedwyn because she realised now that she loved Vivyan Allerton with all her heart.

'I thought I could do it, Alethea,' she explained, when she grew calmer. 'Just as I told you, I'd weighed one thing against another in my mind, and it seemed to me that in the end the things Bedwyn could offer meant more to me than my feelings for Vivyan. I thought I should soon get over those — but, oh Alethea!' She caught her breath on a sob. 'It's like slowly dying inside to watch him flirting with another woman — as he was doing most shamelessly at supper! And then to think of myself having to — to submit to Bedwyn's caresses, when all the time —'

She broke off and shuddered. Alethea nodded in sympathy.

'I can't do it, I won't do it!' Lydia said, vehemently, twisting the handkerchief in both hands as though she were wringing someone's neck. 'Mama may scold me as much as she likes! — and believe me, Alethea, she's going to create the most dreadful fuss when I tell her, for she'd quite set her heart on seeing me a Duchess — but I shan't yield! Not if she thrusts me into a garret, and keeps me on bread and water for years — not for *anything*, I tell you!'

Alethea could not help giving a shaky laugh. 'Well, I scarce think she will be so Gothic as that, Lydia, but I quite see you may have an unpleasant interview in front of you. Can you not enlist your father's support? He was ready enough just now to take your part, and I do think he's very fond of you.'

'True, Alethea, but he seldom opposes Mama, and certainly never in anything that concerns us girls. He has always left our affairs in her hands. No, I see no help in that quarter. There's nothing for it but that I must face up to her myself — and I mean to, don't you fret! She shan't bring me round her thumb this time, and she'd be hard put to it to *force* me to the altar!'

In spite of the appalling scene which ensued on the following day, Lydia's determination never wavered. The original trouble was exacerbated by the receipt of a letter from Eleanor to her mother which of course revealed that Vivyan Allerton had been visiting Harrow at the same time as the two girls. Convinced that this had been deliberately arranged between Lydia and Allerton, Mrs Manbury stormed at her daughter in a way that quite terrified Alethea, accustomed to the calmer reproofs of her own mother. All the same, she felt she must try to defend her cousin.

'Indeed, Aunt,' she put in timidly, 'I assure you Lydia knew nothing of it, just as she says. She was as surprised as anyone when Mr Allerton came to the house with Sir James Devenish and Lady Carteret — truly she was!'

'You may hold your tongue, Miss!' snapped Mrs Manbury, turning on her. 'At least I hope you have acted more sensibly than your cousin! Tell me, did Mr Tracy make you an offer last night?'

Although she was glad to draw her Aunt's fire away from Lydia for a breathing space, Alethea did not relish answering this question. Reluctantly, she admitted that he had; further pressure forced her to say that she had refused him.

'*Refused* him!' shrieked Mrs Manbury, beside herself. 'Refused a most eligible suitor, whom I've been at some pains to throw in your way! Only wait until I tell your mother of this, you ungrateful girl! I don't doubt it's all your fault that Lydia has set her face against Bedwyn — she was pleased enough with the match until you came amongst us — as who wouldn't be, I'd like to know? Fit for Bedlam, both of you, that's what you are! I wash my hands of you!'

Alethea drew herself up with some dignity in spite of a quivering lip, and declared her intention of returning home to Somerset at once. Her uncle later tried to dissuade her from this course, pointing out that his wife's tempers rarely lasted and that Alethea's parents would be offended at her abrupt departure from his house.

'I think not, sir, for I shall tell them how it was, and they'll see then that I could scarce have stayed,' she replied, quietly. 'My mother will, I'm sure, understand her sister too well to bear her any lasting grudge. Indeed, I don't myself, for until today Aunt Olivia has used me with great kindness. I am grateful to you, too, Uncle, for many kindnesses; and ask this one more, that you will arrange for my journey home as soon as possible.'

Seeing the impossibility of making her change her mind, he at length agreed to do this.

'Well, perhaps you are right,' he conceded. 'It may well be that your Aunt would benefit from being rid for a space of the charge of both you girls. After all, she is not as young as she was, and the London season is a monstrously tiring business.

Fatigue may have played its part with disappointment in vexing her with you both. Yes, on mature consideration,' he added, 'I think I shall pack Lyddy off for a while to stay with her sister Caroline, until all this fuss and bother blows over.'

So Alethea returned to the green slopes of the Mendips, the coombes and rivers of her native Somerset where alone she felt she might hope to recover some part, at least, of her former peace of mind.

Chapter XXIII

Alethea crossed a field yellow with buttercups and sweet with the scent of clover, and came to a stile which led into the lane. Here she paused for a moment or two, quietly absorbing the beauty of the day as spiritual sustenance for a still troubled mind. The sky was of that clear, pale blue of summer, with only the faintest wisps of cloud floating here and there on its tranquil surface. Some ducks quacked on a small pond across the way; the stone cottages grouped about it, their gardens bright with flowers, were mellowed by sunshine. It was a day to be happy, she thought, or, if not quite that, to be content. She gave a little sigh, climbed quickly over the low stile, and turned along the winding lane with its high hedgerows in the direction of the Rectory.

The house seemed very quiet as she let herself in, though she could hear the distant shouts of her small brothers playing in the garden at the rear. She poked her head round the door of her father's study. As she had expected, he was sitting there reading, his spectacles sliding down his nose in the way that she found so endearing. He looked up from his book with a warm smile.

'Ah, so you're back, my dear. Is Mama with you?'

Alethea came into the room and closed the door.

'No, she stayed to give Mrs Ponder a recipe and to enquire after her eldest daughter in Bristol. She said I was to tell you she won't be long.'

'Mm, yes,' murmured the Rector. 'That's a pity, for we have a visitor.'

'A visitor?' Alethea was only mildly curious, for a good many visitors came to the Rectory. They were mostly neighbouring clergy or members of their families. 'Anyone of interest, Papa?'

'Oh, yes, decidedly. A most erudite young man, I thought — knows his Sophocles as he ought.'

Alethea nodded sympathetically; a new local curate, she decided. 'Will he be staying to dine with us, Papa? Because if so, perhaps I should give Cook a hint — you know she likes to have plenty of warning.'

'Staying to dine? Well, that rather depends on you, I think. After all, it was you he came to see.'

'Me?' asked Alethea, startled.

'I,' corrected her father, automatically. 'If you remember, the verb "to be" takes —'

'The nominative case — yes, I know,' said Alethea, impatiently. 'But who is it, Papa? Who has come to see me?'

The Rector put down his book and began hunting for something on his desk. 'I have a card here somewhere — now where the deuce — ah! Here it is.' He produced a gilt embossed card and scrutinised it briefly. 'Ah, yes — Devenish, Sir James Devenish.'

Alethea sat down on a chair suddenly. 'Sir James Devenish!' she repeated, in stunned accents.

The Rector surveyed her shrewdly, then smiled. 'Nothing wrong with your hearing, child, is there?'

'Don't tease, Papa! What — what can he want with me — did he say?'

'Oh, yes. He was most explicit. He came to ask my permission to pay his addresses to you.'

Alethea stared at him; some of the colour left her cheeks. 'To — to ask your permission to —'

'Yes, yes. Really, Alethea, your conversation lacks sparkle this afternoon,' complained her father, a twinkle in his eye. 'You do nothing but repeat everything I say to you!'

She sat there as if dazed for a few minutes, then leapt to her feet, her cheeks flaming. 'Papa, he doesn't mean it — he can't be serious! He was only in jest — I *know* he was!'

'Well, I must suppose that you know the gentleman better than I do,' conceded the Rector. 'But it would appear to me that a man who travels a hundred and twenty miles to ask a lady's hand in marriage for sport, must either be intoxicated or out of his wits. I can assert with authority that he was not the former. Would *you* say that he is mad?'

'No — no — of course not! Papa, you're laughing at me, and it's too bad of you! This is serious!'

'Why, so I think, my child. Marriage is a very serious business. And for that reason, Alethea —' his voice took on a more sober note, and again he looked searchingly at her — 'I told the young man that, though he might have my permission to address you, he must take his answer from you alone.'

'I can't believe it!' said Alethea, in a wondering tone. 'It can't be happening — I must be dreaming!'

Her father rose and put his arm about her, gently pinching her cheek.

'There, now you know that you're awake, my dear. And I think you had best go and put the poor fellow out of his misery, don't you?'

She buried her face in his shoulder. 'Oh, Papa, I don't think I can! I feel so — my thoughts are all in a turmoil!'

He kissed her soft hair. 'I know, love. That's something one never forgets. But all the same, you must see him. He deserves no less, whatever your answer may be.'

She raised her head and nodded. 'Yes, of course you are right, Papa, only it was such a shock. Where — where is he?'

'In the garden, playing at cricket with Jack and Billy.'

'*Playing at cricket!*'

'Alethea, pray don't begin again repeating every word I utter! Jack and Billy came to ask me to pitch a ball or two for them, and young Devenish offered to go in my stead.'

'But *Devenish* — cricket!' exclaimed Alethea, dumbfounded.

'I dare say they taught him the game at Harrow,' explained her father, with gentle irony. 'I collect he went there to school.'

Alethea said nothing to this, but peered anxiously at her reflection in the glass door of one of the bookcases.

'I expect I look a shocking fright,' she said despairingly.

'You look lovely — as always, at least to my eyes,' he said, with an encouraging smile. 'I feel sure he will have no fault to find with your appearance. Don't delay longer, my child. And — God bless you.'

She ran to give him a quick hug, then went out of the room.

The Rectory garden was large and rambling, with lawns and flower beds nearest the house, and then a shrubbery which shielded from view an extensive kitchen garden, leading in turn to the stables and a small orchard. The plot of ground allotted over the years to the Newnham boys for cricket practice was situated between the shrubbery and the kitchen garden, too far away from both house and greenhouse windows to cause damage. Alethea made her way there with dragging steps, for although one half of her longed to see Devenish again and hear what he had to say, the other half was ready to sink with embarrassment.

She reached the spot at last to see Devenish, his coat discarded and hung over the branch of a lilac tree, taking a short run before sending down a ball to Billy, who stood with his bat at the ready while Jack crouched in professional style behind the wicket.

Both boys set up a shout of protest on seeing her, knowing at once that it would mean an interruption to their game for some such stupid reason as washing their hands to resume lessons or — worse still — appear in company. Devenish turned quickly, sketched a bow, tossed the ball to Jack who caught it neatly, and went to fetch his coat.

'Oh, Ally, you're a spoil sport!' shouted Billy. 'We were having a famous game!'

'That's no way to address your sister,' said Devenish severely, as he put on his coat and adjusted his neckwear. 'Go on by yourselves, and maybe I'll join you again later — but I make no promises, mind.'

Recovering quickly from their disappointment with the adaptability of their kind, the boys thanked him politely and went on playing.

'Nice lads,' commented Devenish, as by common consent he and Alethea strolled in the direction of the house, and the shrubbery shut off the cricketers from view. 'Show some promise for the game, too.'

'My brother Harry,' said Alethea, in a small voice, 'is accounted quite good — Papa was, also, in his youth.'

'I had a long chat with your father — interesting, too. We broached topics I haven't talked on for years.'

'Yes, he told me — Sophocles.'

Devenish looked at her thoughtfully for a moment. He appeared to be making up his mind. Then he braced his shoulders.

'Did he tell you why I came?' he asked.

She nodded, and the colour crept into her cheeks.

He looked about him. They were walking through the flower garden now; his eye fell upon a rustic bench placed under the shade of a laburnum tree.

'Do you think we might sit over there? I wish to talk to you at some length — if you will permit — and I find perambulation unsuited to my purpose.'

She murmured something in agreement, though she was not quite sure what, and they made their way to the bench.

'That's better,' he said, as they sat side by side. 'Now I can see your face and know what your reactions are to my words. No, pray don't turn your head away, or what guidance can I have? Alethea —'

She turned towards him. He looked full into her eyes for a moment; and suddenly she was in his arms, her lips meeting his with all the pent-up fervour of a long-controlled passion. Presently she drew away, trembling a little. He placed an arm about her, and tenderly stroked her hair.

'I love you, Alethea,' he whispered. 'And it seems you love me — there is the miracle. How soon can we be wed, dearest girl?'

She sat up suddenly, moving away from him along the bench.

'I don't know,' she replied, falteringly. 'I'm not sure — do you truly think we would be wise to marry?'

He looked astounded. 'Wise to marry? Can I be mistaken — do you not return my love? Did your kiss mean nothing? Answer me, Alethea!'

'Yes, I do love you,' she said, in a sad tone. 'With all my heart — far more than I would ever have thought possible —'

He reached out to take her in his arms again, but she put out a hand to ward him off.

'No, pray listen,' she urged. 'We must be quite sure. If that were all — loving and being loved, here and now — then we might find happiness in marriage. But what about hereafter? How long will you continue to love me, and only me?' He opened his lips to protest, but she placed a finger over them and shook her head. 'It's not so long since you thought of me as "a quarry eluding your grasp" — how long will your present feeling for me continue once you have made the kill? Heaven knows I can't bear the thought of losing you, but better now, than find I had lost you to someone else after marriage!'

He had started on hearing his own words repeated, and now he shielded his eyes for a moment with his hand.

'Oh, God,' he said, despondently. 'Of course, I've deserved this! But what can I possibly say to convince you that everything is changed now? Another woman could find the answer in my arms; but that's no way to deal with you, and I respect you for it even while it brings me close to despair! Look at me, Alethea —' his eyes, deep and serious, sought hers — 'don't you understand that a man could become a persistent flirt simply because he is seeking what he never seems able to find? Seeking the one girl for whom he would willingly forsake all others to go hand in hand with her through life? Perhaps I never realised it until I learned to love you, Alethea, but such was my case! And now, when at last my search is ended, it seems my past indiscretions are like to lose me the prize I sought for so long in vain!'

She could not doubt his sincerity. This was not the flippant Beau who could take nothing seriously, but the tender, loving protector who had comforted her during the thunderstorm. And as she came once more to his arms, she thought fleetingly that a future with such an intriguing dual personality was exactly the kind of life that would best suit her own temperament.

She told him so, and was suitably rewarded for her pains.

After a long, blissful interval, she raised her head and sighed 'Poor Lydia!'

'Why poor Lydia, love?'

'Because she's not so fortunate as her cousin — she won't be allowed to marry the man of her choice.'

'As to that,' he answered, 'it's all in a fair way to being settled. I had the story from Allerton — to whom I am eternally grateful, by the way, because it was he who told me you were not, after all, betrothed to Tracy. That information encouraged me to come down here and try to win you for myself.'

'Not knowing you had already won me,' said Alethea, softly. 'And goodness only knows how I managed to keep that a secret from you! But tell me about Lydia, dearest — what happened there after I left?'

'She went to stay with her sister Caroline,' he continued, 'and it seems Caroline put up a strong fight with Mr and Mrs Manbury for Lydia's happiness. Since Bedwyn has obviously cooled off, and there was no further hope in that quarter, your uncle, at least, is in favour of marrying her to Allerton. Vivyan said he didn't think it would be long before Mrs Manbury, too, came round to the notion.'

'Oh, I am so glad! Now I have nothing left to wish for. Except —' she added as an afterthought, looking warily at him — 'except that poor Mr Tracy may get over his disappointment and find someone else to marry.'

'The devil take Mr Tracy! He's caused me enough heart-burnings! Anyway, by all I ever heard, to be crossed in love is the very thing for a poet — it enriches his work.'

'How heartless you are! To think I am to wed such a monster!'

'Heartless — yes — for you have my heart.'

Glancing out of the study window, the Rector saw without surprise that his daughter was held close in the embrace of the erudite young man whose name just now escaped him. He smiled, then sighed. So Alethea would be leaving them. Not so long ago she had been a little doll-like creature climbing on his knee, asking for a story. Now she was a woman, and would have children of her own one day. There was the consolation, he reflected; one lost them, but they were renewed in the grandchildren.

'This were to be new made when thou art old,

And see they blood warm when thou feel'st it cold.'

He sat down again, and reached for his book. Life changed for better or worse, but these old friends — he glanced around his shelves — remained the same.

A NOTE TO THE READER

It's wonderful to see my mother's books available again and being enjoyed by what must surely be a new audience from that which read them when they were first published. My brother and I can well remember our mum, Alice, writing away on her novels in the room we called the library at home when we were teenagers. She generally laid aside her pen — there were no computers in those days, of course — when we returned from school but we knew she had used our absence during the day to polish off a few chapters.

One of the things I well remember from those days is the care that she took in ensuring the historical accuracy of the background of her books. I am sure many of you have read novels where you are drawn out of the story by inaccuracies in historical facts, details of costume or other anachronisms. I suppose it would be impossible to claim that there are no such errors in our mother's books; what is undoubted is that she took great care to check matters.

The result was, and is, that the books still have an appeal to a modern audience, for authenticity is appreciated by most readers, even if subconsciously. The periods in which they set vary: the earliest is *The Georgian Rake*, which must be around the middle of the 18th century; and some are true Regency romances. But Mum was not content with just a love story; there is always an element of mystery in her books. Indeed, this came to the fore in her later writings, which are historical detective novels.

There's a great deal more I could say about her writings but it would be merely repeating what you can read on her website at **www.alicechetwyndley.co.uk**. To outward appearances, our mother was an average housewife of the time — for it was usual enough for women to remain at home in those days — but she possessed a powerful imagination that enabled her to dream up stories that appealed to many readers at the time — and still do, thanks to their recent republication.

If you have enjoyed her novels, we would be very grateful if you could leave a review on **Amazon** or **Goodreads** so that others may also be tempted to lose themselves in their pages.

Richard Ley, 2018.

Sapere Books is an exciting new publisher of brilliant fiction and popular history.

To find out more about our latest releases and our monthly bargain books visit our website: **saperebooks.com**

Printed in Great Britain
by Amazon